FATAL
FICTION

BY

MARY BLOUNT
CHRISTIAN

CB

CONTEMPORARY BOOKS

a division of NTC/CONTEMPORARY PUBLISHING GROUP
Lincolnwood, Illinois USA

MORE THUMBPRINT MYSTERIES

by Mary Blount Christian:

Gory Alleluia
Murder on the Menu

This is a work of fiction. The characters, incidents, and dialogues are products of the author's imagination and are not to be construed as real. Any resemblance to actual events or persons, living or dead, is entirely coincidental.

Cover Design: Larry Didona

ISBN: 0-8092-0673-0

Published by Contemporary Books,
a division of NTC/Contemporary Publishing Group, Inc.,
4255 West Touhy Avenue,
Lincolnwood (Chicago), Illinois 60646-1975 U.S.A.
© 1998 Mary Blount Christian
Manufactured in the United States of America.

890 QB 0987654321

CHAPTER 1

Belinda Mendoza Hill popped two aspirin into her mouth. She forced them down with a swallow of ice water from a paper cup. The water no sooner hit her gums when a sharp pain shot through her, and she shrieked.

Bess, Lin's assistant, poked her head in through the door. "You okay, Lin?" Concern showed on her round face. You never had to guess what Bess was thinking; her thoughts were pasted on her face. She was ten years older than Lin, and she had been at Indeco six years longer. She was very good at her job of assistant. Bess had never misplaced a manuscript. Nor had she forgotten an appointment.

"Yeah. I mean, no, not really. It's that darn tooth I had filled this morning," Lin mumbled. "I forgot, I'm not supposed to have anything cold until tonight."

"Go home, Lin!" Bess said. "You will never have a better excuse to leave early."

Lin pressed a tissue to her mouth. She was still numb enough to drool and lisp from the dentist's shot. How could she feel such pain? Her tongue felt three times its normal size. It kept edging toward the repaired tooth. Clutching her aching forehead between her fingers, she groaned. "I hate Mondays," she mumbled. "I'll vote for the first one who promises to abolish Mondays."

Bess said, "Then I guess I shouldn't mention this."

Lin rolled her eyes. She braced herself for bad news. "Now what?"

"The good news is that the proofs for the book jacket of *Love's Last Chance* came. The bad news is that the heroine's hair is green, not brown." Bess waved a glossy sheet of paper in the air.

Lin whimpered. "We need a good print right away. If it were going to be a black-and-white photograph inside the catalog, it wouldn't matter. But it will be the color cover. That guarantees more attention. More notice means better sales. Call the printer. We need a good proof—and we need it right away."

"Already done," Bess said. "I just thought I would mention it in case you wanted to know where the cover was. The production schedule for the catalog said it was due last Friday. Should I send a copy to the author? I can explain that it's being corrected."

Production schedule. Right. Good, dependable Bess. "No, she's probably not expecting it, anyway. Let's wait for the better copy. If marketing calls about it, tell them—oh, Bess, you know what to tell them," Lin said. She waved Bess away and slouched back into her desk chair. She squeezed her eyelids shut. "I should have stayed in Texas. When I open my eyes, I will be on the beach at Galveston," she murmured.

She wiggled her toes inside her shoes, imagining the

feel of warm sand sifting between them. "Today is all just a terrible nightmare," she said. "I will wake up, and today will vanish." What had Dorothy said in Oz? "There is no place like home. There is no place like home."

Lin had worked hard to get where she was. She was born to migrant farm workers who followed the harvests in Texas. She had never stayed in one school long enough to make friends or complete a grade. Grapefruit in the valley, strawberries south of San Antonio, beans and tomatoes in south central. She had seen a lot of rural Texas in her childhood. She was a teen before she rode an escalator or shopped in a mall. She had studied hard on her own. Mama and Papa had seen to that. She had passed her GED test. With a student loan and a job checking in a grocery store, she had attended college.

"The secret to a good life, little *niña*," Mama told her, "is locked in those books. You must find the key."

At 21 with her college diploma in hand, Lin boarded an Amtrak and headed to New York City. Perhaps being a minority had gotten her the chance at Indeco. But she knew that her skills made her an important part of this small company. She used her skills to work her way up to senior editor. Lin rubbed her throbbing temples. Here, headaches were constant companions.

With ten novels a year her responsibility, deadlines were constant. The worst part about this job was the never-ending meetings. It was either with the art department, the marketing department, or some new writer she wanted to encourage. She loved producing books. She hated meetings.

There were other problems too. Printing machines broke in the middle of printing. Then last month they stitched half of *Mansions of Clay* upside down. They tried to tell her the books would be more valuable as collector's items. Yeah, right. Tell that to the author!

Authors rarely understood the word *deadline*. They were almost always late. Books didn't arrive in time for an autograph party. There was always someone's ruffled feathers to be smoothed. It was tense work.

Most of her authors were easy to work with. They took suggestions and never missed a deadline. A few whined over every suggestion for changes. It was as if they had chipped their stories in stone. Samuel Blessing, for instance. At least she no longer had to worry about his temper tantrums. She had rejected his last book proposal. She hadn't heard from him since. He was probably home sulking.

Her eight-year-old seemed more mature than a few of her authors. With Jeffrey, her worst problem was knowing third grade math. He understood it just fine. She was the one having problems with it.

Jeffrey's biggest fault was never telling her he needed a costume for a play until the night before. How can you make a little kid look like an artichoke? What is an artichoke doing in a school play, anyway?

Of course, there were those manuscripts that arrived without invitation. Stories came in pencil on yellow scratch paper. Writers used typewriters with ribbons that had not been changed since high school. Sometimes Lin thought her eyes would drop out from strain.

Yet she was always anxious to read another story. One of her best writers had come that way, from the "slush pile." Perhaps there was another gem hidden in there. Not always, though. The other day, a murder mystery came with a plastic dagger dipped in catsup. At least she *hoped* it was catsup. You could never tell about the desperate ones.

Once a writer chained himself to her desk, demanding

to meet someone in charge. She introduced him to Roland, the security guard who resembled The Hulk. Tall and muscular, with hair that was so blond it was nearly white, he swooped in like some Nordic warrior and whisked the man away.

Lin glanced around her crowded little cubicle. In her mind she counted off the jobs to be done. Read and reject "slush pile" manuscripts. Read unbound copies of upcoming books for errors. Get the cost estimates for publishing next year's books. Review a couple of contracts. Check the art for a cookbook and . . . Lin stiffened with panic. Schedule! Where was her schedule?

There it was, under yesterday's coffee and half-eaten bagel. She scowled at it.

Lin jumped at the buzz of her intercom, knocking the water into her lap. The wet spot spread across her skirt. "Oh, great!" she snapped. "Just perfect."

Marilyn, the receptionist in the lobby, said, "Samuel Blessing is here."

Lin winced. Why did he have to come today? No wonder he hadn't called. He wanted to confront her in person. She just couldn't handle a scene with Sam. "Tell him—"

Samuel barged into her office. "Tell him yourself!" His voice was so filled with venom and his eyes glinted with so much hate that Lin shrank with alarm.

CHAPTER 2

Lin forgot her pain as she stared open-mouthed at Samuel Blessing. He was not a large man. He was no more than 5 feet 10. Yet his presence filled her cubicle. He roughly shoved a stack of large manila envelopes to the floor and plopped into the emptied chair.

Gathering her wits about her, Lin finally said, "Sam, I have a killer headache, and I just had a tooth filled. I don't need this right now." She knew she sounded wimpish—excuses, excuses. *Take control of yourself, Belinda.* Lin silently cursed the Novocain shot. She had no control over her own tongue. It felt as if it flapped around with a mind of its own. Drool on her chin and the wet spot on her dress were no badges of authority either. *There's no place like home. There's no place like home.*

"Why did you reject my book proposal on the water systems for the Incas?" Sam demanded.

Lin rubbed her temples. This was not helping her headache. She took a deep breath. "Sam, the subject is too narrow; only a handful of scholars would buy it."

"I can broaden the subject. It could be about the Inca cities," Sam said.

"Then it would be no different from others already in print." She shrugged. "Your last three books have not sold well. We are in the business of making money despite what authors think."

Sam leaned forward and glared at her. "So you will just throw me out like a used tissue? You don't promote my books. People don't know about them. How can they buy them if they don't know about them?"

Lin winced. Her tooth was throbbing like a drumbeat. Worse, her head was throbbing with a different beat. "Sam, the marketing department advertises only what they know people will buy. I know that doesn't make sense, but that's the way it is. It's how it was before I came. It will be that way long after I am carted away in a straitjacket."

She shifted uncomfortably. "The warehouse is full of your last three titles. The subjects are so narrow that the audience is limited. They will be remaindered soon, and you will be free to buy them at cost. Then you can market them yourself—if you know how better than our department."

Sam leaped to his feet. "Sell them myself? I am an author, not a salesman." He squared his shoulders indignantly. "It's beneath me!"

Lin shuffled some papers on her desk and picked up her blue pencil. She hoped Sam would take the hint. When he didn't, she said, "Be happy with what you have accomplished. They were wonderful books, or I wouldn't have bought them. I have to show a profit, or I am out of a job. If your brother's books didn't sell so well, my list would show a loss."

She immediately regretted mentioning Ben. She shrugged helplessly and waited for the scene that would surely come. It did.

Sam swiped her desk clean with his arm. He leaned over until he was almost nose to nose with her. "Leave Ben out of this! I hate Indeco Publishing. I hate New York City. And I hate you! But most of all I hate Ben! His novels are trash! Pure trash!"

Lin rolled her chair back so that her legs were not under her desk. How far was it from her chair to the door? If Sam came after her, would she be able to get around him? Could she leap across the desk and avoid him? Cautiously, drawing no attention to herself, she slipped out of her heels. She wished she were wearing her jogging shoes.

The security guard Roland poked his head in. "You wanted to see me?" He looked at Sam suspiciously. Roland was six feet tall or more. He could look as sweet as a teddy bear or as stern as a grizzly bear. Just now he was wearing his grizzly look.

Lin shook her head, relieved. "No, Roland, but since you're here, please show Sam out."

Roland put one hand on Sam's shoulder and guided him toward the door.

Sam turned to glare at her. His eyes looked wild. "You've seen the last of Ben. I'll see to that! He will never publish again! You and Ben will be sorry. *Very* sorry!"

When they had left, Bess rushed in with a cup of coffee. "Good grief, Lin! I never heard Sam act like that before."

"You never heard him rejected before," Lin said. "Do you think he can talk Ben into leaving Indeco? Would

Ben do that just because Sam says so?"

Bess shrugged. "I don't know what either of those guys will do. Twins can be kind of weird, I think. You know, all that time growing in the same womb. And then looking at somebody who looks just like them. Weird. I just don't know what he'll do. Be careful."

Lin rubbed her jaw; it felt swollen twice its normal size. She must look like a chipmunk gathering nuts for winter. "I should have insisted on the contract saying Ben had to give us his next book. Maybe I did. Check his contract, Bess." She took a sip of the coffee and sucked in her breath. She was supposed to have nothing hot, nothing cold, until tonight. Why couldn't she remember that? "What do you think he meant by 'Ben will never publish again'?"

Bess shrugged. "He was in a nasty mood; that's for sure."

Lin said, "Maybe I should call and warn Ben." She reached for the phone on her desk. She had called that number so much, she knew it by heart. There was no answer.

Bess said, "Sam will cool off by the time he gets back to that quaint little farm of his. Go home. Nobody should be here after being in a dentist's chair all morning."

Lin stooped to pick up the envelopes that Sam had scattered on the floor. Pain shot through her head like a bullet. Even her eyelashes hurt. She grabbed the chair arm to keep from tumbling head first onto the floor. "Oh, you're right, Bess. I'm doing no one any good by staying today. I'll take the Martin manuscript home to work on. Maybe by the time I get home, I will feel just fine."

"Don't count on it," Bess said.

"Thanks for your support," Lin replied grimly. She stuffed the manuscript into her briefcase. The room was wobbling, or was she? "If anyone calls—"

"I'll tell them you moved to Bora Bora." Bess grinned. "Hurry up and get out of here before another angry author finds you."

Lin signed out and rode the elevator down to the lobby. She stopped briefly to thank Roland for coming to her rescue.

"Thank Bess," he said, wearing his best teddy bear expression. "She was the one who told me a maniac was after you."

"That's a bit dramatic for what really happened," Lin said. She hesitated, then asked, "Did he say anything else when you walked him out of the building?"

Roland laughed. "Only that he hated me, you, and everybody else. He was mumbling something about taking Benny's wife somewhere or other. I was just trying to move him out the door, so I didn't pay too much attention. I won't let him in anymore, Ms. Hill."

"Hmmm," Lin replied. "I didn't know Ben was married. Take her where?"

*   *   *

Usually Lin walked the mile to the subway entrance. In her tennis shoes, it wasn't bad. She considered that her exercise for the day. Today, every step she took sent shooting pains into her mouth and head. Worse, she now had a giant water stain on her lap. She had that funny feeling on the back of her neck. It was as if everyone were staring at her.

They weren't, of course. In New York City, you could paint yourself hot pink and nobody would look twice. It was so crowded, people created their own little private worlds. Heavens! Today the beep and blare of the traffic rattled her teeth.

She sighed wearily and hailed a taxi. That turned out to

be a lousy idea. The cabby dodged through stalled traffic, slammed his brakes, and blasted his horn. Lin felt worse than before. She choked down another aspirin without the benefit of a glass of water. That was yet another bad idea. The taste clung to her throat like chalk dust.

Lin paid the cabby and hurried down the steps toward the subway platform. Bess was right to suggest leaving the office early. Being bumped by a herd of thoughtless, rushing people was no way to travel today.

She backed away from the platform edge and leaned against the wall, feeling a bit sleepy. Had she taken only two aspirin? She couldn't remember. The track clattered, and the subway train squealed to a stop. The doors opened with a whoosh. She stumbled inside. A few people were already aboard, reading their *Times*, typing on laptop computers, or dozing. At least there were no boom boxes in this car.

Lin chose an aisle seat in the middle of the car and spread the contents of her briefcase on the inside seat. She hoped the car would not get crowded so she could keep the seats to herself. Lin yawned. She felt the urge to nap, but what if she missed her stop? Anyway, a subway car was no place to let down your guard.

Her eyelids fluttered as she fought to stay awake. Through the haze she thought she saw someone on the platform staring at her. There, by the pillar, that man looked familiar. It was Sam! He was leaning against the pillar with his arms crossed, glaring at her. Was he following her?

She blinked hard and looked again. There was only an old woman with shopping bags. She had to get control of her imagination.

Lin made a special effort to stay fully awake and aware. What did she really know about Sam? She tried to remember.

He had taught English literature in a small-town college, hadn't he? Why didn't he still teach? With tenure, that job was much more secure than writing. It took something drastic to get fired from a college. That temper of his, perhaps? What had he done? And to whom?

Wasn't his college job why he wrote those scholarly books? Professors' Rule Number One: Publish or perish. He needed publishing credits in his personnel file. She knew exactly what he made from his books. He couldn't live on that. He would have been a fool to quit the college.

For twins, Sam and Ben seemed as if they were from different planets. Sam was uptight and formal. He wrote books about interesting but little-known wonders of the world that only libraries bought.

Ben was talkative and fun-loving. He wrote novels that were as trashy as they came, and they sold in the millions. Never underestimate the public's interest in trash. That's what made Ben a bestseller. That's what made Lin a good editor. She understood the pulse of the public.

Had the college fired Sam? Why? She had never asked. Had he threatened someone at the college? Lin made a mental note to learn more about her authors from now on. Roland said that Sam had muttered something about taking Benny's wife. But Ben had no spouse that she knew of.

Ben and Sam shared the farm they inherited. What if Roland heard wrong? What if Sam said *life*, not *wife*? She tried to shake the cobwebs from her head. She was letting the bad scene at the office get the best of her.

Samuel Blessing was out of sight; he should be out of mind. He would cool off and be embarrassed at the whole thing by morning. He would even send one of his stuffy little apology notes. Good-bye, Samuel. What a blessing to be rid of Samuel Blessing!

She giggled loudly as the doors swished shut, and the

subway car lurched forward. Suddenly aware that a few passengers were staring at her, she said, "OOPS, that's not me; it's the drugs. I mean . . ."

Passengers looked away from her. Lin slumped back into her seat. She felt her face grow warm. This time it was embarrassment and not fever. "It's only aspirin," she mumbled.

She could forget all about Sam. At least, she hoped she could. However, would Sam forget about her? Her eyelids fluttered shut. She tried blinking them open. There was something she needed to tell Ben. What was it that she was supposed to tell Ben? A word from her childhood popped into her mind: *peligroso*. She could almost hear her mother's voice saying, *"Peligroso, hija, alto*. Dangerous, daughter, stop."

CHAPTER
3

Lin grabbed her briefcase and purse and worked her way to the exit. She pushed through onto the platform and hurried up the steps. The sun was so bright she squeezed her eyes shut a moment. Blinking until her pupils adjusted to the brightness, she was surprised. "Mom?"

Mom was Mrs. Hill, her former mother-in-law. Although Lin's marriage had been a disaster, two good things came out of it: her son Jeffrey and her in-laws. She and Jeffrey lived on one side of a duplex in Queens, and the Hills lived on the other.

Her ex lived in California with his computer job and his new wife. Gerald was a better ex than a husband, so their divorce was successful. She sometimes teased him that she got custody of his parents in the divorce. The Hills took care of Jeffrey after school, and that saved her a bundle on day care.

Many people were surprised that she chose to live so close to the Hills. They never offered advice unless she asked for it and they never snooped. Mom even encouraged Lin to date again, but who had time to meet new people? The church had singles socials, but Lin usually didn't go. Jeffrey was her main concern now. Jeffrey and her job.

"Mom, what a surprise! What are you doing here?" Lin asked. "Not that I'm sorry to see you." She tried to smile. She wasn't sure if it worked; her lips were still pretty numb.

"Bess called," Mrs. Hill said. "She said you were coming home early. I thought you could use a ride home." She took Lin's briefcase and gently guided her by the arm.

"Bless Bess," Lin said. "And bless you."

They walked to the car, and Lin got in and closed her eyes. She could relax now. Mom would take care of her.

*   *   *

Lin must've fallen asleep. The next thing she knew, they were home.

"Sleep it off," Mrs. Hill told her. "I'll keep Jeffrey after school, just as if you were still at work. I'm making chicken and noodle soup. We'll bring some over later. By that time, you'll be in tip-top shape."

Lin yawned. "You are a darling. Thanks." Lin let herself in, kicked off her shoes at the door, and flopped across the sofa. Rouster, the gray tabby cat, leaped on her stomach. "Ouch!" Lin said. "It's time to get your claws cut again, silly animal."

Rouster settled into a ball, purring. Lin wanted to scold him, to run him off, but she could feel herself falling asleep. She didn't wake until Jeffrey was leaning over her, calling to her.

Mom came through the door with bowls of steaming chicken soup. She had already set the table with placemats and glasses of milk.

"Wow," Lin said. She rubbed her eyes. "It's dark already. And I feel like a human again. Sore, but human." She gave Jeffrey a hug and asked about his day.

"Ms. Joseph gave me an A on my essay on Benjamin Franklin," Jeffrey said. He waved the paper in front of her.

"You *earned* an A on your essay," she said. "Ms. Joseph doesn't *give* anything that isn't deserved." She mussed up his hair.

Benjamin Franklin. Benjamin. Lin frowned. What was she supposed to do about Benjamin Franklin? No, Benjamin Blessing. That was it. The fog in her head was beginning to clear. She needed to call Benjamin Blessing.

"You two enjoy the soup," Mom said. "Knock on the wall if you need anything." She left.

"*Sopa*," Jeffrey said. He made a slurping noise.

Lin grinned. "*Sí*, soup." She let the warm soup trickle down her throat. She was glad that Jeffrey wanted to learn Spanish. He picked it up easily. She waved her spoon.

"*Cuchara*," Jeffrey said, as if on cue.

"*Bueno*, good," Lin said. She and Jeffrey ate their soup while they made plans for the weekend—shopping for tennis shoes, the Tigers' Little League soccer game, and church. Lin smiled. When she was traveling around Texas with her parents, brothers, and sister in that rickety old truck, she had never dreamed little Belinda Mendoza someday would be a soccer mom.

When they finished, Lin said, "Do your homework. I'll clean up." She took the empty bowls into the kitchen and turned on the hot water. She held her fingers under the running water. When it ran warm, she plugged the sink and squeezed a little liquid soap into the swirling water. Should she call Ben tonight or wait until morning?

If she called him tonight, it might sound like a warning instead of just information he should know. But it was a warning, wasn't it? Sam was really angry. At her. At Ben. She couldn't get his angry face out of her mind.

She rubbed the soapy dishrag around inside the bowls. She held them under the running water to rinse. Sam would cool off by the time he got back to the farm. She could talk to him tomorrow. She might even suggest more popular subjects for him to write about. After all, he was an expert researcher and a good writer. *Yes,* she decided, *that's what I'll do. Tomorrow.*

Lin checked over Jeffrey's homework. While he took a bath, she sat on the sofa and wrapped herself around a throw pillow. She watched an old comedy rerun on Nickelodeon. These old black-and-white comedies were fun to watch. She was glad that Jeffrey liked the old comedies best. She smiled to herself. Jeffrey was a good kid. She reached over the arm of the couch and picked up a framed photograph.

It was from three years ago. She and Gerald were still married. Jeffrey had her dark brown eyes and Gerald's strawberry blond hair. It was a striking combination. It reminded her and Gerald that Jeffrey was a joint responsibility. That was about the only thing that she and Gerald agreed on. Although Gerald was in California, he was still very much a part of Jeffrey's life. That's the way it should be.

Lin replaced the photo as Jeffrey scrambled onto her lap. She groaned under the weight. He was getting big. He was wearing his rocket-ship pajamas. He smelled of soap and toothpaste. She hugged him. "Okay. Off to bed with you. I'll tuck you in and read another chapter tonight."

They were reading *Charlotte's Web.* Jeffrey could read it for himself. But she liked reading to him, and he liked being read to. It was a nice connection, one she didn't want him to outgrow soon.

After she had read to him, she turned out the light and treated herself to a bubble bath before bed.

*   *   *

Lin was startled awake by the ringing of the bedside phone. She groped for the phone and the lamp switch at the same time. As she answered, the caller hung up. Lin glanced at the clock. It was 2 A.M. It must've been a wrong number. But who would call anyone at this hour of the morning?

She turned off the light and pulled the covers up around her chin. Just as she drifted off, the phone rang again. She got it by the third ring this time. Whoever it was hung up at the sound of her voice.

When this happened the fourth time, Lin was fully awake and angry. She dialed *69 for call-back. She half expected to hear music or a party in the background, some half-drunk idiot who couldn't dial for a taxi or home.

"Hello?" It was a gruff male voice. It was a familiar voice.

Lin pulled the receiver away from her ear. She stared dumbly into it as if she could see the caller. She didn't need to see, though. Her skin crawled up her spine, tingling. She knew who it was.

"Sam?" Lin said. "How did you get my home number?" It was unlisted. Only her co-workers, the school, and a few friends had it.

"Who?"

"Don't deny it, Sam. I know it's you."

"Who is this?"

By now Lin was really wide awake and ready to strangle him. "You know very well it is Lin."

"Why are you calling me at this hour of the morning?"

His voice was as snappish as she felt.

Lin gritted her teeth. She spoke slowly, deliberately. "Sam, I used the call-back code. It returns the last call made to this line. There is no mistake. You have been calling me every few minutes and hanging up. So don't play games with me. It won't work."

There was a pause. "It must've been Benny. He is very angry with you, Lin. He doesn't like the way you treated me."

Lin's fingers tightened around the phone. "I am sorry, Sam, but I don't believe you. Do not ever, *ever* call this number again, do you hear?"

There was a click, then a buzz. He had hung up in her ear. She returned the phone to the cradle. "This certainly clears my conscience about you, Samuel Blessing. I won't be giving you any ideas for books after all," she said.

Lin resolved to have her number changed. She sighed. No, there would be too many people to notify. She would surely forget someone. But she could get caller ID first thing tomorrow. The way she understood it, it recorded the name, number, and time of a call. Then she would have proof. If Sam persisted, she could report him to the phone company.

Lin turned off the lamp and fell back onto her pillow, exhausted. Her eyes popped wide open. There would be no more sleep for tonight. She might as well work on the Martin manuscript. But tomorrow or later this morning, she would call Ben. He should know about his brother's strange behavior. He should know that she was very annoyed, maybe even a little frightened of Sam.

Lin sat up in bed. A horrible thought came to her. If he could find her phone number, what was to stop him from finding her home address? Lin shivered at the thought. *"Peligroso,"* she whispered. "Dangerous."

CHAPTER 4

Lin felt sluggish as she entered Indeco the next day. Her body felt heavy, as if it couldn't fight earth's gravity. She must have looked no better than she felt.

Marilyn, the receptionist, looked up from her work as Lin got off the elevator. "You look awful!"

Lin shrugged. "Thanks for your concern," she said grimly.

Heads turned, faces grimaced as she walked toward her office near the back. It was a rat's maze of sharp turns. She always felt as if a piece of cheese should be waiting for her when she got to her office.

"Oh, my!" Bess said. "You look—"

Lin held up her hand. "Don't say it. Just don't say it. And get me Benjamin."

She stopped and turned toward Bess. "Sorry, I didn't mean to take my night out on you."

Bess's voice dripped with sympathy. "Your tooth?"

"No—Sam. Did you ever give him my home number?" She tried to sound casual, not accusing.

Bess's expression was one of shock and horror. "Of course not! Never! Not in a million years. I—"

"Oh, I know, Bess," Lin said. "But he did get it. And he was calling me and hanging up in the early hours of the morning. I feel— I feel like leftover mashed potatoes."

Bess made a face. "Eu-u-u! You poor thing. I'll bring you coffee. How about a granola bar to go with it? I have some with cranberries."

"Just the coffee, thanks. And make it black. But first, call Benjamin. I need to get this over with." Lin slumped back in her desk chair, waiting.

Bess came in with a cup of coffee. The steam swirled around like a miniature ghost. "Sorry, Lin. There's no answer. I'll keep trying."

Lin held the coffee under her nose and breathed deeply. "Okay. I really need to talk to him. But not Sam. I don't want to talk to Sam under any circumstances." She took a long, soothing sip of coffee, then sighed.

Benjamin had a book manuscript due by the end of the week. She decided to ask about the manuscript. She would remind him of the due date. Then she would mention Sam. That way she wouldn't alarm Ben, but she would let him know. They were twins. He should know.

Lin shuffled papers on her desk. At times she glanced through the door toward Bess's desk. Bess shook her head no. Still no answer. Lin called the phone company and ordered the caller ID service. Then she walked around and stuck her head into the cubical next to hers. Brad Benton was leaning back in his chair with his feet on his desk. He was reading a manuscript and chuckling to himself.

"New humor book?" Lin asked.

"No, not intentionally," Brad said. "Listen to this. 'Blossom pushed her way through the prickly hedge with no thought of the scratches on her soft, ivory arms. She heaved herself into the muscular arms of Heathcliff, paying no attention to the sharp medals awarded him for heroism that adorned his broad manly chest. Her ruby lips quivered with excitement.' "

Lin grinned. "Ouch! That's really bad!"

"Yes, but it made my day," Brad said. "It's manuscripts like this that keep me going. I like to visualize what the author looks like."

"And this author?" Lin asked. "What do you see?"

Brad's face seemed to relax as he drifted into his imagination.

Lin cleared her throat. "Did you give Samuel Blessing my home phone number?"

Brad frowned. "We all stick together on that. Nobody gives out anybody's number; you know that. Why?"

"Because I was called last night by Samuel Blessing. Between 2 A.M. and 4 A.M. A lot! First hang-up calls. Then when I challenged him, he claimed it was his brother."

Brad leaned forward. His face expressed worry. "That sounds psychotic, Lin. That's harassment. You should turn him in. Report him."

Lin frowned. "I'm not sure he's dangerous, but I have a child to worry about. If Sam knows my home phone number, he may know where I live too."

"Definitely report him!" Brad said.

"Right now, it's my word against his. But I ordered caller ID. Then I will have proof," Lin said.

"Not necessarily. Not all those little long distance

companies show up with numbers. It might just say 'out of area.' "

"I never thought of that," Lin admitted. "Maybe Sam didn't either. He's such a snob, he probably uses only the top of the line service."

"You can get a tracer put on your line," Brad suggested. "Call the phone company."

Lin nodded. "If it happens again, I will. I did tell him never to call again. And the calls stopped. I hope that means he has stopped for good."

She asked everyone in the office if they had given out her number. No one had. She remembered the receptionist had her number too. She walked through the security door into the lobby across from the elevator. "Marilyn, did you give Sam Blessing my phone number when he was here?"

Marilyn made a face. "I wouldn't give him *my* number, even if I were desperate for a date. That guy scares me." She reached for her address carousel. "Now his brother is a different matter!" She flipped to the *H*'s. Frowning, she said, "Your card is not here. I'm sure I had it. But it's gone now."

Lin felt the skin snake up her spine. "Do those cards have our addresses too?"

Marilyn nodded. "Yeah. I don't understand how it could be gone."

"Never underestimate an angry author," Lin said. She hurried back to her desk and dialed. "Mom, I don't want to scare you. But if you hear any noise in our apartment, don't go to check. Just call the police." She hesitated. "And, Mom, be at the bus stop a little before Jeffrey is due. If there is a stranger hanging around—"

"Lin, is everything all right?"

"I'm not sure." She took a deep breath. "It's probably

nothing, but I just— Just promise me you will be alert. Tell Dad too, okay?"

There was a pause. "All right. I'll tell him. But when you come home, you come to our apartment first. We'll go in together, right?"

"Right, Mom. Thanks." Lin hung up just as her intercom buzzed. She flipped the switch. "Yes, Bess?"

"I finally have Ben on the phone." She paused. "At least he says he's Ben."

"What?"

"I mean, he says he's Ben. But Lin, he sure sounds like Sam to me."

The temples in Lin's forehead throbbed. Now what? "I'll take it," Lin said. "They do sound alike. Either way, I'll talk."

Lin picked up her phone. She decided to see if she could trick him. "Sam?" she said. "Sam, is that you?"

There was a pause. "No. This is Ben. Why would you say Sam?"

Lin bit her lip. She wished she could be sure. There was an edge to the voice, a sound of superiority. There was an impatience. That was Sam's way. Ben was gentler sounding. He always sounded as if he took life lightly. Sam sounded as if he were fighting life. She decided to play along but with caution.

"Ben, has Sam talked with you?" she asked.

"Yes. I am very angry with you, Lin."

Those had been Sam's exact words in the wee hours of the morning. She felt pretty sure this was Sam, not Ben. Well, she could play the game too. "Ben, you have a manuscript due, according to the contract. I wanted to be sure it is arriving on time."

This time the pause was longer. "I am very angry with you, Lin."

"Even so, er, Ben, you have a contract."

"What about Sam? Brothers should stick together. We should support each other."

Peligroso, that voice whispered in her head. Dangerous. "Sam is a very talented writer. I am sure he will find a more suitable publishing house. One that knows better how to market his special talent."

The voice was calmer now. "We should be together. We should be in the same publishing house. Just like here at the farm."

"After you finish this book with us, I will consider releasing you, Ben," Lin said. She didn't want to. He was a real money maker. Surely she could straighten things out with the twins.

"Sam hates me," Ben said. "And it's your fault." There was an edginess to his voice. At that moment she was sure that she was talking to Sam, not Ben. But where was Ben?

Her intercom buzzed. Lin flipped on the switch. "Bess, I'm on the phone with—"

Bess's voice sounded frightened. "It's Jeffrey's school. You better take this."

Panic shot through Lin. Without thinking, she clicked the current call off and tried to calm her voice. "What is it?"

It was the principal. "There is a man here who wants to take Jeffrey out of school a little early. But he's not on the list you gave me. I asked him the password you gave us. He doesn't know it. He says he's Jeffrey's father. I—"

Lin's body went numb and cold. "No!" she said. It was as if her heart had leaped into her throat. "No! Call security! Do it now!"

CHAPTER
5

Lin dropped the phone to the floor. She grabbed her purse, knocking papers helter-skelter. With any luck, she could get a cab immediately. She could get to the school in maybe half an hour.

A muffled voice shouted from the receiver. "Lin? Lin, don't panic. It's me!"

She dropped back into her chair, trembling. Grabbing the phone, Lin shouted, "Gerald? What are you doing here? I thought—What are you doing in New York?"

"I was on a business trip to Canada. I have a six-hour layover. I wanted to be with Jeffrey. I'm sorry I frightened you."

"Well, you did!" Her voice snapped. She swallowed hard. "You should have called here first."

"I know that now. You remember, I'm not always the most thoughtful person in the world."

"Yes, I remember. You say you have six hours?"

"Yes. I wish it were more, but Kiki is expecting me back this evening."

Lin made a face. Kiki. How could anyone take seriously someone named Kiki? "Which airport are you flying from?"

"LaGuardia."

"Then take Jeffrey with you when you go to the airport. I'll take a cab out there and meet you before flight time. That'll give you two more time together. Call your parents. Mom is expecting Jeffrey on the bus. I don't want her scared when he doesn't show. You hear?"

Gerald's voice sounded subdued. "I hear. I will call. Sorry, Lin."

"Let me talk to Mrs. Johnston. I'll tell her you can get Jeffrey."

"Thanks, *mi corazón*," Gerald said. "You're the greatest."

Lin shook her head, disbelieving. *Mi corazón?* Sweetheart? The only Spanish he ever learned, and it was no longer appropriate. "Gerald, don't ever do this again, okay?"

"I promise. I said I was sorry, Lin. Okay?"

Lin explained to Mrs. Johnston that Gerald's visit was a surprise. "However, I am very glad to talk to you. I appreciate your concern. I am worried right now about someone who might try something. If anyone besides myself or the Hills asks to see Jeffrey, call security immediately. Don't wait to talk to me."

Lin hung up the phone. She realized she was still shaking. She felt ice cold.

Bess came in. "Jeffrey sick? Do you need to go?"

"He's fine. Gerald is in town. He wanted to be with Jeffrey awhile."

Bess heaved a sigh. "Ah, I was scared for a minute that Sam—"

Lin held up her hand. "Don't even say it. I feel shaky enough already. Bess, I plan to work through the lunch hour so that I can meet Gerald and Jeffrey at the airport later. How about ordering corned beef sandwiches and cartons of milk from that little place down the street?"

"It's Tuesday," Bess reminded her. "They have chili today."

"Just corned beef for me," Lin told her. Chili in New York City might as well be boiled chicken. Nobody knew how to season it the way she grew up knowing. *Muy picante!* Very hot to taste. There were Tex-Mex restaurants opening up in various areas of New York. They were the rage, but their food was nothing like home. It wasn't chili unless it burned all the way down.

*   *   *

Lin checked out of the office at 3 P.M. She took a cab to the airport and checked the Delta flights to San Francisco. Gate 27. Gerald and Jeffrey were deep in conversation when she reached the waiting room. There were shopping bags at Jeffrey's feet. The boys had been shopping. Good. She hoped there were some jeans in there and not all video games and model cars.

"Thanks for the time with Jeffrey," Gerald said. "It's unbelievable to see how big he has grown since last summer. The photographs just don't show how much."

Lin smiled. "Our Jeffrey is smart too. He did send you his grades in his last letter, didn't he?"

"Yeah. I just wish I wasn't so far away, that's all."

"That's where your work is. That's how it is. Soon he will be with you for the summer. Then *I* will be the lonely one." She gave Jeffrey's hand a squeeze and smiled at him.

The first call for boarding was announced on the speaker.

Gerald said, "I'll wait. There's still plenty of time. I wanted to ask you something, Lin. Is everything all right? You kind of scared me today. And Jeffrey said you were warning him about strangers again this morning. It sounded like more than the usual warning. What's up?"

Lin frowned at Gerald. She didn't really want to talk about Sam in front of Jeffrey. There was probably nothing to it. Why scare the boy? "Jeffrey, there is a soft drink machine right over there. Here, take these quarters and get yourself something. And come straight back," she added.

"Lin?" Gerald said when Jeffrey had left.

Without taking her eyes off Jeffrey, she told Gerald briefly about Samuel Blessing. "It's probably nothing. I just want to be sure, that's all."

"I can cancel my flight. I can stick around a few days until you're sure," Gerald said. "I can stay with my folks."

Lin shook her head. "You have a new life, Gerald. With Kiki." She winced slightly at the sound of the name. "I have a new life too. We will be all right. But thanks. I am not afraid. I can take care of myself—and Jeffrey."

She hoped she sounded braver and more convincing than she felt. But it was true. This was something she had to work out for herself, independent of Gerald. They were not a family anymore.

Jeffrey returned with a canned drink as the last call came over the speaker.

Gerald reached to give him a big hug and shoulder pat. He straightened up and looked at Lin. "Call if you need anything—anything, understand?"

Lin squeezed his hand. "Understood. And thanks." As an afterthought, she said, "Spring break begins next week. Why don't I send Jeffrey out this weekend?

That'll give you two weeks together."

Gerald quickly agreed. Jeffrey hugged Gerald good-bye. Lin shook his hand. *My, how civil we are*, she thought. *How very civil.*

They watched through the window until the plane had lifted off and disappeared into the sky. Then they headed toward the taxi stand on the floor below.

"Mom, are you and Dad worried about something?" Jeffrey asked on the way home. "You want me out of town. Was it about all those calls last night?"

Lin turned toward Jeffrey, amazed. Whoever thought they could hide anything from a child? She explained about Samuel, leaving out as many details as she could. "I think he is sick, Jeffrey. But he will be all right. So will we."

"By the time I get back from California?" Jeffrey asked.

"I promise!" Lin said. "Two weeks, and everything will be just fine."

Jeffrey seemed satisfied. He was no doubt preoccupied with thoughts of the trip, his first alone on a plane.

Lin leaned back in the taxi and relaxed. Everything would be just fine. She knew what she had to do. As soon as Jeffrey was safely on the plane, she would do it.

CHAPTER 6

When Lin's taxi turned onto their street, she felt a hard knot tighten in her chest. Two blue and white squad cars were in front of their duplex. The lights on top were flashing. Several uniformed officers were walking around the yard.

"Stop here," Lin told the driver. She searched the crowd in the small front yard. There were Mom and Dad. They didn't look hurt. She paid the driver and helped Jeffrey out of the back with his packages. Taking his hand, she hurried toward the house. Her knees were wobbly. Her lips felt numb. Her head was swimming. *Don't pass out*, she told herself. *Don't panic, not yet. It could be anything. A gas leak. An escaped robber. Don't jump to conclusions.*

One of the officers stepped forward. "Sorry, ma'am. You can't come past this tape. This is a crime scene."

Jeffrey's eyes were wide and dancing. He held her

hand so tightly Lin felt the circulation slowing down. "I live here. What happened?" she asked.

He lifted the tape. "Then we have questions to ask you, Mrs.—?"

"Hill," Lin said. "Belinda Hill. This is my son Jeffrey. We live there. Why is my door open? Mom? Dad?"

Mrs. Hill looked up, relieved. "Lin!" She rushed forward and gave Lin and Jeffrey reassuring hugs. She straightened up. "We did just as you said, Lin. We heard noises and we called the police. What is this all about?"

The officer said, "It seems like a case of vandalism. But we will need you to check. Tell us if anything is missing." He took Lin's arm and guided her through the crowd of officers with notebooks and cameras.

"Jeffrey, stay with Grandma," Lin said. She took a deep breath and stepped inside the apartment. "Oh, no," she whimpered. "Look at this! Just look at this! Why?"

The sofa pillows were slashed and feathers scattered about. Pictures were ripped from the wall and their glass shattered as if someone had stomped them with his heel. Drawers were open and their contents dumped to the floor. Dishes were smashed.

Tears welled in Lin's eyes and spilled to her cheeks. "Why?" she repeated.

"It doesn't appear to be teen vandalism. They usually raid the fridge and drink up the soft drinks, beer, anything that they feel like. It doesn't seem to be robbery either. Your TV is still here and your computer too. This has the look of anger, real anger," he said. "The other Mrs. Hill said that you had called her to be alert for something like this. You were expecting it?"

Lin picked up the photo of herself with Gerald and Jeffrey. Carefully she removed the pieces of glass from it.

"Not exactly. I'm an editor. One of my authors is angry at me. An ex-author," she corrected.

"You think he might do this?"

Lin shrugged. "I don't know, but maybe. He did make phone calls to the house—lots of them in the middle of the night."

"Were they threatening calls?"

"No, he would hang up when I answered."

"What makes you sure it was him, then?"

"I dialed call-back. He answered right away."

"Does he live near here?"

"No, he lives upstate. I can't believe this." Lin wrote down Sam's name, address, and phone number. She handed it to the officer.

He frowned at the paper. "His address is out of the county. We have no jurisdiction. I will alert the police there. But the prefix of this phone number—those are assigned to wireless phones. He could've been calling you from anywhere. Even across the street."

Lin grabbed her throat. She closed her eyes, and the vision of Sam's furious expression was there. She shook as the reality hit her.

"Your father-in-law said he will change the lock before we leave. The old one wasn't very secure. However, don't stay here tonight. Get what you will need and stay with them. A squad car will patrol this street. The officers will keep an eye out for anyone hanging about."

Lin looked up. "Do you think he might come back?"

The officer raised one eyebrow. "Don't you?"

When Mr. Hill returned from the hardware store with a new bolt lock, the officers left. It was late. "Dad, I'm going to leave this mess tonight. I haven't the heart to clean up. I'll just get a few things for myself and Jeffrey. If you'll lock up when you're finished, I'll worry about this tomorrow."

"You should call your insurance company. Let them see the damage after you have listed everything that was destroyed."

Lin glanced around the room. Broken glass, ripped pillows, scattered feathers. She was sure it wouldn't even add up to the deductible. In a way, she felt almost sorry for Sam. Even in his anger, he wasn't very effective.

Or was he? "Rouster?" Lin called. "Here, kitty, kitty." She'd never forgive him or herself if he had hurt a poor innocent cat. "Rouster!"

The cat slithered from under the sofa. His eyes were wide with terror. Lin scooped him into her arms and smoothed his fur until he purred. "Poor Rouster, poor kitty. You must've been terrified." She gave Rouster an extra treat of chicken with gravy for his trouble.

Lin gathered her own clothes for the next day and then went into Jeffrey's room. Oddly, it hadn't been damaged. Perhaps Sam loved children. Or perhaps he didn't have time. She frowned. Something was different. Something was not quite right, but what? Lin froze. A large stuffed bear was usually leaning against the pillows of Jeffrey's bed. It was gone. Lin looked under the bed. She looked all around. It was definitely gone. A stuffed bear, so large that it wore an old outfit of Jeffrey's.

Lin shivered uncontrollably. Was this a signal to her? Was Sam trying to tell her something? Lin whispered her son's name. "Jeffrey. My darling Jeffrey. May guardian angels watch over you."

She hastily grabbed socks, underwear, a shirt, and pants from the chest. Lin fled her apartment and hurried to the Hills'. "If Jeffrey didn't have important tests in school, I'd send him to Gerald tonight. But we must watch him. We must be careful," she told the Hills.

"They should arrest that man," Mrs. Hill said. "They should throw away the key."

Lin shrugged. "There is no proof that he did this. There is only a possibility."

"It's a very good possibility, though," Mr. Hill said. He handed her the shiny copper key to her new lock. He clipped the other onto his own key ring.

"What about fingerprints?" Mrs. Hill asked.

"That's almost a myth," Lin said. "I've edited enough crime novels to know that fingerprints are nearly impossible. Layer after layer of prints cover each other. They'd have to fingerprint everyone who has ever been in the apartment. Even then, it isn't too likely that they would find the right prints. They won't go to all that trouble and expense for minor vandalism."

Lin was aware of her phone ringing in the night. She could hear it through the wall. The caller gave up around 4 A.M. She lay there listening.

After getting Jeffrey off to school, she left a voice mail for Bess explaining that she would be late. Lin and the Hills went next door and cleaned up the glass and feathers. She threw the pillows out. She re-hung the pictures although she didn't replace the glass. She only hoped that Jeffrey would be too excited about his trip to notice that his bear was missing.

*   *   *

At work, Lin checked her incoming mail. Ben's manuscript was due Thursday. It was usually early. If it was at least on time, she would be happy to forget the past week. But if it didn't show up . . .

Lin kept to her schedule of editing, meetings, and

begging salesmen to push her books in the bookstores. Much of what she was doing was routine. She couldn't keep her mind off Sam and Ben Blessing. Thoughts of them crept into her mind like cold air under a door. Something was wrong. She was sure of it. Which was worse? Sam's anger and harassment, his vandalism—if it was Sam—or his silence? When he was silent, she couldn't help but wonder if he was thinking of more bad things to do.

She tried all day Wednesday to talk to Ben. Either there was no answer or Sam answered and made excuses. "He's not here." Or "Ben is in the barn." Or "Ben went to town." She didn't mention the break-in and vandalism. Yet the thought of it hung in the air as she spoke. Each time she called, she asked Sam to have Ben call her when he returned. She never heard from him.

"He tried to call," Sam said. "Your line was busy." Or "You were out." Lin didn't believe him for a second.

*   *   *

Thursday, Ben's manuscript didn't arrive. She decided to change her tactics. "I will come out there. I will pick up the manuscript," she told Sam.

"No!" he said. "Ben doesn't feel good."

"What is the matter with him?" Lin wanted to know.

There was a pause. "I don't know. Just sick."

"Call the doctor then," Lin said. "Don't let Ben lie without medical help."

"He doesn't want a doctor," Sam said.

"When people are sick, they don't always think clearly. Call the doctor," Lin insisted. "If you don't, I will."

"Yeah," Sam said. "I will."

Lin called early Friday. "How is Ben?" she asked.

"Ben is worse. Much worse," Sam said.

"Did you get the doctor?" Lin wanted to know.

"Yes, sure. But Ben is worse."

Lin had an uneasy feeling. "What did the doctor say? Who is the doctor?"

Sam's voice raised a pitch. "Why do you ask?"

Lin tapped her desk with her pencil, annoyed. "Just interested, that's all."

"Dr., er, Dr. Randall. He said Ben is very sick."

Lin frowned. "That doesn't sound like a professional diagnosis to me. Sick with what?"

Sam hung up.

Lin returned the phone to its cradle. Something was wrong out there. She was sure of it. Ben was in danger. What did the courts call it? Reckless endangerment? Wanton neglect? Perhaps she should call the local police to investigate. She dismissed that. What could she say? Instead, she decided to call the physician. As an interested friend she could ask about Ben without suspicion.

Lin hit the intercom button. "Bess, get the number of a Dr. Randall in Potash. I don't know his first name. Potash is just a hole in the road, not even on the map. There shouldn't be more than one Dr. Randall there."

In a few minutes, Bess came in. "There is no Dr. Randall in Potash. I had the long distance operator look for one in nearby towns. There is no Dr. Randall anywhere unless you count the veterinarian."

"I was afraid of that," Lin admitted. "Please call the car rental agency. I'd like a semi-compact car Sunday—early. I have some vacation time coming. I'll use it to clear this up while Jeffrey's in California."

Bess's eyes widened. "You're going there? Lin, you ought to think about this more."

Lin rubbed her chin slowly. "I have been thinking a lot. Bess, have you ever heard the old joke about the man who calls home and is told that his cat has died?"

Bess shook her head. "I don't think so, Lin. Why?"

Lin frowned. "Briefly, he calls home and inquires about the family. His brother blurts out that his favorite cat has died. The man is shocked, and he tells his brother that he should have broken it to him more gently. When the brother asks how, the man says, 'The first night you could have said the cat was on the roof.

"'The next night you could have said the cat was sick. The next night you could have said it was worse. And then the last night you could've said that the cat had died. That way it wouldn't be such a shock.' The brother says he understands. So the man calls the next night to inquire how things are going. His brother says, 'Grandma is on the roof.'"

Bess grinned. "That's funny, Lin, but what has that got to do with—"

Lin leaned back in her chair and sighed. "Bess, I can't shake this really bad feeling. I am afraid that Ben is on the roof."

CHAPTER 7

Lin sat with Mom and Dad in the bleachers as they watched Jeffrey's Little League soccer game early Saturday afternoon. She and Jeffrey had spent Friday evening packing his bathing suits, tennis shoes, T-shirts, and shorts for his trip to California. He would be leaving after today's game.

Lin tried to concentrate on cheering Jeffrey's team. She tried, but she was a dismal failure. Thoughts of Sam reached out like fingers and clutched at her, choking out other thoughts. Lin glanced around the bleachers. Was he lurking about?

"You seem nervous, Lin," Mr. Hill said. "Are you thinking about that man?"

"Calling in the night and slashing pillows are acts of a coward," Lin said. "I am not afraid of him." She wondered if Dad knew she was telling a little white lie.

The police had told her that the vandalism showed he

was becoming more angry. He could become worse. She was glad that when the game was over, she could put Jeffrey on the plane. He would be safe in California. She was determined that their lives would be back to normal by the time he returned in two weeks. Facing up to Sam was the best plan she had. Lin wished she had one she was more confident in.

She had not yet told her plans to Mom and Dad. Did they suspect? she wondered. Dad would certainly insist on going with her if he knew. This was her fight, though.

The cheers caught her attention. "Two, four, six, eight! Who do we appreciate? Tigers, Tigers, Tigers!" Lin clapped and waved at Jeffrey. He ran into their team huddle. The coach praised them loudly for a good game. He handed them each a canned drink.

The three Hills climbed down from the bleachers and waited for Jeffrey to join them. His face was red with excitement. "Did you see me, Mom? Did you?"

"Great play," Lin lied. She had no idea. Her mind had been miles away in Potash.

Mr. Hill drove by the apartment so that Jeffrey could clean up and change. Lin put the luggage into the car trunk. They all drove to the airport. While Mr. Hill parked, Lin and Mrs. Hill checked Jeffrey's luggage and got his boarding pass. They walked him to his gate and sat waiting for the boarding call.

Mr. Hill soon joined them. He had stopped at the newsstand and had several comic books in his hand. Lin wasn't particularly happy to see the comic books, but she knew that she gave Jeffrey plenty of good books too. He knew the difference.

Lin left to speak to the flight attendant. She explained that this was Jeffrey's first flight alone. Lin pulled a photo of Gerald from her purse. "This man is his father.

He, and only he, should take Jeffrey off the plane. I am trusting you to take care of Jeffrey and see that no harm comes to him."

The attendant's badge said her name was Joanna. She smiled and rested her hand on Lin's arm. "I take care of children traveling alone every day. I will take good care of him."

"Yes, but . . ." Lin's voice trailed off. She was about to say something about Sam. Instead she smiled. "Yes, but Jeffrey is mine."

"I will board him personally," Joanna promised. "You may go on board until we're ready to leave if you like."

"Yes, I would," Lin said. When Jeffrey had said good-bye to his grandparents, Lin held his hand and followed Joanna down the ramp and into the plane. She watched everyone who came aboard. She knew she had no reason to be uneasy, yet she was.

Satisfied that Jeffrey was safe aboard and under the watchful eye of the attendant, she kissed him good-bye and got off. She waited with Mom and Dad until the plane shrank to a dot and disappeared. *"Vaja con Dios, hijo,"* she whispered. "Go with God, son."

Relieved that Jeffrey was out of harm's way, she felt lighter. On the way home she said, "I will be gone by the time you get up tomorrow. I have rented a car. I plan to go to the country a little while, take a few days off work."

"That's a good idea. We'll look after things here. If you're going to be on the road alone, then you must take our cell phone," Mrs. Hill said. "You might need to call."

Lin looked at her. Did she know? Or was she just being careful? She didn't argue. "Thanks, Mom. I'll be fine. But it is nice to have a phone."

Mrs. Hill gave her the phone when they got home. "It's charged and should last your trip all right. Here is the plug to recharge it at night, just to be safe. And here is the plug that will fit into the cigarette lighter in the car."

Lin told them good night and promised to call. She called Gerald to give him Jeffrey's flight number and time of arrival. "Call me when you have Jeffrey there, okay? I'm going to Potash where Sam lives tomorrow," she told Gerald. "I didn't tell Mom and Dad. But I wanted you to know." She didn't add "just in case."

From the tone of Gerald's voice she knew he heard her unspoken words. "I can't talk you out of it?"

"No."

"Then good luck, and be careful. Don't see him alone, you hear?" Lin laughed. He sounded more concerned now than when they were married.

As promised, Gerald called her as soon as the plane landed. Jeffrey was full of excitement about his first ride alone. His voice bubbled on the phone. "They gave me a pair of wings to wear; they are just like the pilot's!"

*   *   *

Early the next morning, Lin threw a small bag of necessities into the front seat of the rental car and set the cell phone within arm's reach. Neither hot nor cold, it was a good day for a pleasant drive. She only hoped the destination was as pleasant.

It was nearly lunchtime when she arrived in Potash. If not for the small sign and a few buildings, she might have passed through it and never known. Lin stopped for lunch at the only cafe. It was small and old. The linoleum design was worn away in the heavy traffic areas, but the walls looked recently painted. While she waited for the waitress to bring her Reuben sandwich and tea, she called Sam. She did not tell him she was in Potash.

"How's Ben?" she asked.

Sam paused a minute. "Ben is dead."

Lin felt her body go numb. "Dead," she repeated. "How?"

"I—I told you Ben was sick. I warned you he was very sick. It's terrible. Dr. Randall said there was nothing he could do."

Lin snapped to attention. "Dr. Randall, you say? Are you sure that's his name?"

Sam's voice was hesitant. "Yes. Randall. Why? Don't you believe me?"

"Of course, I do," she said. "I—I had just forgotten his name, that's all. I should come, Sam. I should pay my respects. When is the funeral?"

"No funeral!" Sam shouted. "No, don't come!"

"No funeral! What do you mean, no funeral? Won't the townspeople want to pay their respects? Won't they want to support you?"

"No funeral," Sam repeated. "No funeral. Ben didn't want one. He hated funerals. He made me promise."

"No memorial service, either?" Lin asked. As a child she had been taught to respect the dead. She and her family always returned to their birthplace near Laredo on the Day of the Dead. They cleaned the family graves and washed the gravestones and brought flowers. They remembered and respected the dead. *Maybe not all cultures do that*, she thought, *but surely all of them honor their recent dead.*

Lin said, "I'm terribly sorry about Ben. It must be even harder on you, considering your harsh words recently."

There was a pause. "What harsh words?"

Yeah, right, she thought. *What telephone calls, and what vandalism too.* Lin tucked the phone back into her purse and motioned to the waitress. "Do you know of a Dr. Randall around here?"

The woman tucked her pencil behind her ear. "Yeah, the vet? He's about three miles down the highway."

"No," Lin said. "A doctor for humans."

The woman shook her head. "Naw, nobody by that name." She looked over her shoulder toward the kitchen. "Jake!"

A round-faced man stuck his head in the pass-through. "Yeah?"

"We got a Doc Randall here—one that tends people?"

Jake shook his head. "I guess Randall could treat someone in an emergency. He might like treating somebody that didn't bite." He withdrew, laughing.

"Is there a funeral home in town?

The woman frowned at Lin. "He won't do animals."

Lin tried to keep the frustration out of her voice. "Is there a funeral home?"

"The next town. We don't have but 250 people in all of Potash. Maybe you ought to talk to Doc Adams. He's the doctor for people. And if they don't get well under him, he's also the coroner. Convenient, huh?"

"I suppose," Lin said. "That's one way of looking at it. Where might I find this Doc Adams?"

"It's a brick house. Red brick with green shutters. About a block back. He doesn't have a sign out front because we all know it's the Doc's. And he doesn't want to be advertising drugs to addicts who are traveling through town."

Lin thanked her. The woman was obviously annoyed at the questions. Some small towns are like that. They close ranks and protect their own. Was anyone protecting Ben?

Lin paid her check and turned to leave. "You didn't mention a constable or a sheriff. You do have one, don't you?"

Sighing wearily, the woman said, "Just a deputy assigned by the county. He's usually fishing at the lake. But if you want to talk to him, try back here around five. That's when he comes in to eat."

Lin reviewed what little she knew. A deputy who spent his time fishing. Probably some old geezer whose only job was to ticket travelers for missing that one stop sign in the road. She might want to ask him to go with her to the Blessing farm. But first she had to be sure that Sam wasn't just lying to her. He had sounded so peculiar.

Her first stop should be to see the doctor, also known as the coroner. When she faced Sam, she wanted to be prepared. She wasn't sure anymore why she was pursuing this head-on. Did she want to cause Sam trouble for vandalizing her apartment? Was she more worried about Ben than angry at Sam?

All she could think about was that missing stuffed bear wearing Jeffrey's toddler suit. She was doing this to assure herself that her son would be safe from this guy. She had to do this, no matter what the consequences. *Peligroso*, that voice whispered. Dangerous!

CHAPTER
8

Lin drove to the red brick house with the green trim. She had passed it on the way into the village of Potash. She was not even sure this place would qualify as a village. It was more like a populated rest stop on the country road. Lin stepped onto the narrow porch and rang the bell. A buzzer sounded and the lock slid with a clank. She pushed the door and entered a small room that looked more like a parlor than a waiting room. There was no one there.

A swinging door squeaked open. Through the opening came a hand holding a knife. Lin's mouth flew open in a scream. She backed toward the door.

"Oh, sorry," the man said. "I was making my lunch." A smear of mustard was on his upper lip.

Lin hadn't realized she was holding her breath until she let it out in a wheezing cough. She tried to calm her breathing. She forced herself to look away from the knife to the man's face. He was young, perhaps her age, with a boyish friendliness that might have been charming had he not still been holding the knife. Auburn-haired and green-eyed, he had freckles generously sprinkled across his face. Right now they seemed to blend into just one; he was blushing. *Boyish charm*, she thought.

"I'm sorry. I didn't mean to frighten you. I'm not performing horrors in my laboratory. Have you eaten?"

"Y-y-yes," Lin said. "Go ahead. Don't let me keep you from your lunch."

"I'm Ric Adams," he said, extending the hand without the knife. "The townsfolk call me Doc Adams. It's supposed to be some sort of joke because of an old TV western or something."

Lin nodded. *"Gunsmoke.* I caught the reruns. I'm Lin Hill."

He laughed. "Guess I had my nose in med books at the time." He motioned to her to come into the room. "I can offer you some hot tea. Sure you don't want anything to eat? I mean, I'd put off lunch and be the good doctor, but you look good to me." He blushed again. "I mean, pretty healthy. I figure you can wait, right?"

Lin laughed. "I'm not here for medical help. I need information."

He carefully placed a lettuce leaf on a slice of bread, then the thin-sliced chicken, then another slice of bread, and cut the sandwich diagonally. "You know I'm bound to my patients' right to privacy," he said. "Never rat on a patient; my mentor taught me that." He grinned at her, showing a row of even, white teeth. "Sit," he said, pulling a chair from under the small table. He poured them each a cup of the tea.

Lin nodded her understanding. "I think you can at least tell me if someone was your patient."

He thought about it for a moment. "I suppose there's no harm in that."

"Benjamin Blessing?"

Ric Adams frowned. "Nope. Not one of mine. Of course, I've only been here a year."

"You're sure?"

He said, "Oh, yeah. It's real good experience. It's mostly setting broken bones and sewing up cuts. And there are occasional gunshot wounds. Some fool forgets to unload his hunting rifle and shoots himself in the foot. It's a small town. It's lousy trying to make a living here because they are all disgustingly healthy."

Lin shifted her weight impatiently. "I meant, are you sure you don't know Benjamin Blessing? You are the coroner too, aren't you? Aren't you required to pronounce someone dead before they can be buried?"

He stared out the window a moment. "Blessing, Blessing. I recall a Blessing but not Benjamin."

"Samuel?"

"Could be. That sounds right. But I'm not sure."

"But no Benjamin?"

"No Benjamin. That I'm positive about. And certainly not lately."

"There's no other physician? A specialist, perhaps?"

Dr. Adams laughed. "There's not enough for me to do in general practice, let alone a specialist. I'm just waiting out the end of my contract with the town council, and I'm out of here. If they didn't guarantee me a monthly minimum, I couldn't afford this sandwich!"

Lin sipped her tea, thinking. Samuel had told her a Dr. Randall treated Ben. But the only Dr. Randall was a veterinarian. This doctor had never treated Benjamin. He said he hadn't even heard of him. In a town this small, surely they had run into each other at some time.

"Benjamin is of medium build, light brown hair, about 50 years old. He is an extrovert if ever there was one."

"Doesn't ring a bell," Dr. Adams said. "This guy looks like everyone here. Middle-aged and average. But an extrovert? He'd stand out big in a town full of recluses. It's hard making friends here. Sometimes I think I'm invisible."

"I know he lives in Potash," Lin said, exasperated. "At least he lived here. His brother said he died."

Dr. Adams looked up from his sandwich. "Here? He must've been in a hospital, not here."

"All I know is what I was told," Lin said. "His brother said he was very ill. He said that Dr. Randall—"

Dr. Adams frowned. "Dr. Randall is a vet!"

"I know that!" Lin said. "I'm only repeating what Sam told me."

"Look, if you are suspicious about this guy, maybe I'm the wrong person to talk to," Dr. Adams said. "Maybe you should be talking to the deputy instead."

Lin sighed. "I intend to. But the waitress said that he was fishing until supper."

Dr. Adams laughed. "I'll let you in on a little secret. He doesn't fish. 'Gone fishing' is his way of keeping folks from bothering him about tracking down some driver who backed over their mailbox, or somebody's cow that broke through a fence. He can disappear and study."

"What if it's more than a bent mailbox or stray cow?" Lin asked. "Can't they disturb him then?"

"Oh, sure. We're very up to date in Potash. We page him."

Lin doubled her fists in frustration. "Then page him, please! I don't want to be stuck here after dark with no place to sleep but my car."

"Sorry, Ms. Hill. I guess not everyone finds this place as amusing as I do." He wiped his mouth and walked over to his wall phone. He dialed and hung up. "Incidentally, there is a bed and breakfast about five miles up the road. You can't miss it—an old house with a cannon in front."

He grabbed his phone on the first ring. "Amigo," Dr. Adams said. "Sorry to disturb your *fishing*, but there's a young woman here who is very anxious to talk to you." He held out the phone to Lin. "Deputy Manny Alvarez at your service," he said. He returned to his sandwich as soon as Lin took the phone.

"Deputy Alvarez," Lin said. "I am very concerned about the well-being of an acquaintance."

"Why?" the deputy asked.

Lin glanced at Dr. Adams, who seemed busy completing his lunch. "He has missed a deadline. I have repeatedly called. First his brother wouldn't let me talk to him on the phone. And now the brother tells me he is dead. The brother has been harassing me, and he's threatened my son, sort of." Tears welled in her eyes as the thought of Jeffrey came to her. She knew she must sound hysterical by now.

Dr. Adams turned in his chair to look at her. He poured her a glass of water and handed it to her.

"Stay at the doc's. I'll meet you there," Deputy Alvarez told her. "About five minutes."

Lin gulped down the water. She took a deep breath. When she was a little girl, Mama would kiss away her tears and tell her that her guardian angel was there watching over her. Lin hoped that the deputy would prove to be a guardian angel. She figured it wasn't this boyish doctor with a mustard mustache.

CHAPTER 9

Lin jumped as the buzzer rang. Dr. Adams wiped his mouth and crumpled his paper napkin into his plate. "Duty calls," he said. He pushed a button near the kitchen door. "You might be more comfortable in the waiting room. Manny should be here pretty quickly. When he gets here, bring him back here to the kitchen. No one will disturb you here."

Lin touched above her own lip and cheek. "You might want to get rid of the mustard before you see your patients," she said.

"Thanks," he said and grinned that charming grin again. He quickly washed off his face at the sink, then opened the door between the kitchen and waiting area. Lin nodded her thanks and walked into the waiting room. A woman sat there hugging a little girl to her, rocking slightly in the chair.

"Sinuses acting up again, Amy Lee?" Dr. Adams asked.

He placed a hand on the girl's shoulder. "Well, come on in and let's see what magic I have for you."

The two followed him into a room across the hall. Lin picked up a two-year-old *Vogue* magazine from the side table. Typical. What did doctors do? Scavenge garbage dumps for old magazines? All the styles that were supposed to be so ahead of their time had been discarded by now. She tossed the magazine aside, wondering about the deputy. Manny Alvarez. Was he a Texas-born Latino too? This backwoods area of upstate New York seemed like an odd place to find someone of Hispanic heritage.

The bell sounded. She heard the clank of the bolt lock and stood, ready to extend her hand and meet Deputy Alvarez.

Lin stared open mouthed. The man stood at least six foot six. From his broad chest and well developed arm muscles, Lin figured he worked with weights. His skin was the color of dark chocolate. His hazel eyes seemed to bore right through her.

"Something wrong?" he asked.

"It—it's just with a name like Manny Alvarez I wasn't expecting—That is, I—"

Deputy Alvarez laughed heartily. "You weren't expecting anyone of African ancestry. I get that a lot. My father was from Puerto Rico. My mother was Jamaican. I might add that from a name like Hill, I wasn't expecting anyone of Latino ancestry."

"My ancestry I got from my parents. Hill I got from my ex-husband," she said.

They both laughed as they shook hands. "Dr. Adams suggested we talk in the kitchen," Lin said.

Manny Alvarez swung open the kitchen door, and the two of them sat at the table. "Now start over, please, and tell me why you are worried about this person you mentioned on the phone."

"I'm an editor in a publishing house," Lin began.

"No kidding!" Manny interrupted excitedly. "I'm taking a correspondence course on writing."

"Oh, well, as I was saying, the Blessing twins were both on my author list. I couldn't use any more of Sam's manuscripts but I kept Ben. I think Sam got insanely jealous of his brother Ben. I know he got furious at me. He made a terrible scene at the office. And then he wouldn't let me speak to Ben on the phone. He told me Ben was sick. Then he told me Ben died."

Manny shrugged. "People do get sick and die, Ms. Hill. There's nothing suspicious about that."

Lin hit the table with her fist. "You aren't hearing what I'm saying! Sam is dangerous, I'm sure of it! He broke into my apartment and vandalized it. He harassed me on the phone. And I think he threatened my child."

"You *think* he threatened your child? You're not sure?"

Lin's voice quivered with frustration. "He—he stole the teddy bear from my son's bed. It was dressed in Jeffrey's toddler clothes. I believe he meant that as a message, a threat."

Manny Alvarez rubbed his eyes. "A teddy bear? You consider that a threat to your son?"

"Yes! Subtle, yes, but yes, I consider it a threat."

"And that's all you have to go on, Ms. Hill? Was he arrested for B and E?"

"B and E?" Lin asked.

"B and E: breaking and entering. Was he arrested?"

"Well, no, there was no proof that he was the one. But I'm sure it was Sam." Lin could feel her body tensing. "He told me that Dr. Randall treated Ben. Dr. Randall is a veterinarian. Dr. Adams has not seen Ben, not as a doctor or a coroner. Now that tells me that either Ben is alive and may need help, or he's dead and—and—Sam may have killed him in a fit of jealousy."

Deputy Alvarez chuckled. "I think you are reading too many mysteries, Ms. Hill." He leaned back in his chair and drummed his fingers on the kitchen table. He pursed his lips and focused his eyes on the corner of the room, frowning. Lin fidgeted in her chair, waiting until she thought she would scream.

He at last broke the silence. "The NYPD did not suggest a restraining order because of the scene at the office?"

"They said that was too uncertain." Was this deputy buying any of this? she wondered. "Don't you know the Blessing brothers? They're twins. I should think that would be unusual enough in a place so small as Potash," Lin said.

"Twins?" Deputy Alvarez echoed. "I can't say I'm aware of twins around here. Grown ones at that. Of course, if they weren't in the same place at the same time, maybe I didn't pay any attention. Especially if they don't make trouble. Everyone pretty well minds their own business here. Mind yours, and they don't pay any attention to you. Tell you what I'll do. I'll fax some of the law enforcement agencies in surrounding areas to see if this Ben Blessing was admitted to a clinic, or died and was buried, or even if they've had complaints. Meanwhile, I'll pay a little visit to this Samuel Blessing, see what he has to say for himself."

"I'll go with you," Lin volunteered. Surely Sam couldn't deny anything if she was standing right there in front of him.

"I don't think that is a good idea, at least not yet. Your presence could set him off if he's as unstable as you say.

Are you planning on staying close by, or you heading back to the Big Apple?"

Lin shrugged. "Dr. Adams told me about a bed and breakfast. I'll try there for tonight."

"Ah, yes. Thelma's. Nice little place. Then I'll call there later. If Thelma doesn't have any room, there's a motel another five miles beyond. I'll find you. And I'll look into this for you, Ms. Hill."

Lin looked up as the door swung open. Dr. Adams walked in. "Everything squared away now?"

Lin stood and offered her hand to Dr. Adams. "Thank you for your hospitality." She turned toward Deputy Alvarez. "I'll be expecting your call. Thank you."

The two men walked her to the front door. Lin stepped onto the porch. She looked back, half expecting the deputy to walk out with her. His four-wheel drive with the police star on the side was parked next to her rental car. He nodded good-bye and lingered behind, talking with Dr. Adams. Maybe he wanted an opinion from the good doctor about her sanity. She was beginning to think she should have left well enough alone.

"Since Thelma serves only breakfast, we'll probably see you at the cafe this evening," Dr. Adams called after her. "Tonight's apple cobbler night."

Lin stopped a giggle. He was such a little boy at heart. "Great," she said. "See you then."

Deputy Alvarez hurried out to the car and held the door for her. "Maybe while you're here you could look at some of my stories," he said. "Give me a professional opinion."

"Oh. Great," Lin said. She hoped it didn't come out with the same tone she felt. One more budding author. Does everyone in the world have a story to tell? She just hoped that Ben still did.

CHAPTER 10

Lin drove north toward Thelma's bed and breakfast. To the right of the road she saw a row of rural mailboxes. A gravel road intersected with the farm road. Slowing down, she read the names on the boxes: Hayslip, Marsh, Collins, Blessing.

She was tempted to turn down the road and face Sam that very minute, demand to see Ben. She didn't believe for a second that Ben was dead. This was just Sam's way of keeping her from seeing him. What if he was holding Ben against his will? Perhaps he was hoping that she'd give up. *Well, I've got news for you, Sam Blessing. I'm stubborn and determined, or I wouldn't have gotten where I am today. I am not giving up!*

Lin laughed to herself. And where *was* she today? Alone on a two-lane farm road, far away from her own safe bed. Alone, looking for answers that would help her get rid of a psychotic who was making her life miserable. Alone. Oh, how she hated that lonely word.

In childhood, when she, her sister, and her brothers were stacked in their rickety old truck, she yearned to be alone. When the family of six shared a one-room migrant shack on a strange farm, she dreamed of being alone. In those communal showers on the farms, she longed for her very own tub. Now she knew: alone was not all it was cut out to be. She pressed the accelerator and met the 45 mile an hour speed limit. She passed signs that warned of deer crossing, of slow tractor traffic, and finally one that announced one mile to Thelma's.

Thelma's was obviously as old as the Revolutionary War. It was pockmarked with musket ball holes in the whitewashed walls. It looked as if little had been done to the outside except painting. The windows, too, were original. They reflected the landscape in a wavery pattern like the house of mirrors in the amusement park. A state historical marker and a wooden sign in Old English lettering announced the bed and breakfast.

Lin parked and rang the bell. A woman with a flour smudge across her cheek answered. "Miss Hill?" she asked.

Lin recovered her surprise. "Uh, Ms. Hill, yes. But how—?"

The woman wiped her hand on a towel and offered it to Lin. "Rachel Penobscott," she said. "Deputy Alvarez called to tell me to expect you."

Lin smiled. "That was thoughtful of him." She gazed about the room. From the pegged wooden floors to the high ceilings, the place looked untouched by more than a broom and dust cloth since it was built. It must have been considered almost a mansion in its early days. Pewter candelabras sat on the high mantle. Portraits of long-dead patriots and finely dressed ladies decorated the painted clapboard walls. It was a bit like stepping back into the past.

"Let me just cover my dough to rise," Rachel said. "Then I'll show you to your room. Come with me, if you like. The kitchen is the only room in the house, except the bathrooms, of course, that has been modernized."

Lin followed her through a cozy dining area into the kitchen. It was bright and clean with stainless steel appliances and a tile floor the color of buttercups. The only part left from the original kitchen was a massive fireplace with copper utensils and a cast-iron pot on a metal arm.

"There," Rachel said. "There'll be cinnamon rolls and mini quiches for breakfast in the morning. There're only two other guests right now. I've taken the liberty of inviting Deputy Alvarez and Doc Adams to join us at breakfast tomorrow."

Lin smiled. "Thank you. Has anyone ever done a photo-documentary of this place for a book? I think it would be a wonderful introduction to architecture and home life in the 1700s."

"My, no," Rachel said. "It's like a lot of places scattered about the rural areas. We do have a couple of postcards, though. One shows the outside, and the other shows the parlor."

"Have you lived here long?" Lin asked.

"All my life. My mother was Thelma. She died about five years ago."

"You know the people around here then?"

"I guess I know just about everyone. My mother served full Sunday meals, reservations open to the public. So at one time or another, just about everyone has eaten here. I went to school here, too, at Consolidated."

"You know the Blessings?"

"I knew Robert and Sarah Blessing. And their son Samuel, of course. That is, I knew him before he went off to college. He is a famous author, you know. I don't understand a thing he's talking about or care for his subjects. But I'm sure he must be brilliant." Rachel laughed. "At least according to him, he is!"

Lin laughed. "What about Benjamin?"

"Who?"

"Benjamin Blessing. You must know him too!"

"No, can't say that I do." Rachel washed her hands over the sink and dried on a paper towel. "Now let me show you to your room. The kitchen is open between 6:30 and 10 A.M. After that—" She shrugged. "After that, you're on your own. The coffeepot stays on, and any leftovers will be in the refrigerator."

She led Lin up a narrow wooden stairway and into a hall with the same white wooden walls as downstairs. Here, too, portraits of men and women of another age lined the walls. Lin's room had a four-poster bed covered with a colorful patchwork quilt, a chest of drawers, and a spool-style rocking chair. The lamp on the chest, although it looked like an oil lamp, had been changed to electric.

Lin glanced at her watch. She should return to the cafe. Perhaps Deputy Alvarez had something to report by now. She smiled to herself. And of course, there was that famous apple cobbler! "I am not sure what time I will return this evening," Lin told her. "I don't want to wake you or the other guests."

"Oh, glad you mentioned that. Here. This is to the outside door, and this is to your room. And if I don't see you until breakfast, have a good night's sleep. There are two bathrooms on this floor serving the three bedrooms, one at each end of the hall. Use either one. I suspect one of the gentlemen will want to escort you back here. If you'd like, bring them into the parlor. I know them both, and I trust them to be gentlemen."

When Rachel left, Lin unpacked her small bag. Hairbrush, shampoo, toothbrush, and toothpaste—these she placed on the chest. Her pajamas, robe, and slippers she laid out on the bed. She put her underwear and jeans and T-shirt into the drawer. She hoped she would need to stay no longer than her clothes would last. Perhaps there was a public laundromat nearby.

When she was settled, Lin went down the steep wooden steps. She ran her fingers along the rough wall. Several holes with the metal of a bullet still showing were scattered along the stairs. The battle for this patriot property had actually come inside, she realized. Mentally, she imagined such dramatic shots in a book. If only Sam weren't such a jerk, she could have him do it. But no, she was finished with him.

*   *   *

Lin drove toward the cafe. From the corner of her eye she glanced at the row of mailboxes once more. She slowed the car and pulled to a halt, biting her lip. Should she? Probably not, she thought. *Peligroso*, dangerous, that voice whispered.

Lights winked at her through the dense stand of trees. They reminded her of the fireflies from her childhood. She used to twirl and dance among them and pretend they were fairies come to rescue her from her dreary life. Her dancing sent them scattering, and she skipped after them, calling, *"Alto! Alto!* Stop! Stop!" But they flitted away into the night, leaving her to dream alone.

Lin sighed. As the sky turned concrete gray, the lights seemed brighter, stronger. They beckoned to her. She ignored the warning voice in her head and turned down the gravel road. Pebbles pinged against the car. The tires made a scraping sound as they stirred up the loose gravel. She wouldn't go in. She would just drive by. She would not even slow down. Sam would never know she had been around. But she was curious about the Blessing farm. He spoke of it as if it were a huge estate. She had seen it in her fantasies. She imagined her family living on such a place, living there permanently, not traveling from farm to farm, picking someone else's fruits and vegetables. Her father had had that dream before he died, worn out and disappointed at 53.

Lin slammed on the brakes as the rear passenger window shattered. She must have dislodged a rock somehow. It had hit the window just right. Lin was glad she had taken the insurance clause in the rental agreement. She would hate to buy a new window. They were probably pretty expensive.

The smell of burning wood filtered into the car through the opening. She looked up. Smoke curled up from a chimney on a mouse-gray house just ahead and to the right. It was hardly a cool night. Why would anyone be using a fireplace tonight? No matter. That broken window had dampened her adventurous spirit. She turned the car around and headed back for the main road and the cafe. Perhaps Deputy Alvarez or Dr. Adams could find some plastic for her to cover the window until she could get it repaired.

She arrived at the same time as Deputy Alvarez, and they parked side by side in the lot. "What happened to your window?" he asked.

"Oh, I hit a rock, I think. I shouldn't have gotten off the main road." Lin immediately regretted mentioning that. It was like a confession.

He frowned. "You went to the Blessing farm?"

"Oh, no!" Lin protested. "That is, I drove on that road. I didn't stop. I was curious."

"Don't do that again," he said. His voice was sharp. He immediately softened. "That is, it isn't wise to go there alone, not until all of this misunderstanding is straightened out."

Lin choked back a laugh. "Misunderstanding? Is that what it is?"

Deputy Alvarez got his flashlight from his jeep and opened the door on the side of the shattered window. He stuck his head inside the car. "We can use some heavy plastic and duct tape on this window. I've got a whisk broom in the jeep. Let's get this glass out of here before—"

Deputy Alvarez rubbed his fingers along the leather seat back. He pulled out of the car and looked at Lin, frowning. "You say, a *rock* hit the car?"

Lin shrugged. "I didn't see it, but it must have been. Why? What else?"

He took her by the shoulders and looked her straight in the eyes. His expression was grave. "Because, Ms. Hill, there is a bullet lodged in the seat cushion."

CHAPTER 11

Lin felt her face grow numb. Quickly the numbness drained into her body. Her legs wobbled, unable to hold her up. "Sam," she whispered.

Deputy Alvarez steadied her. "Don't jump to conclusions, Lin. May I call you Lin? Ms. Hill seems so formal. Call me Manny, please."

"He knows I'm here," Lin said. "Is my conclusion a jump? It's not even a small step! Sam is the only one hereabouts who knows me. Sam and Ben, and you and Dr. Adams. It wouldn't be anyone but Sam."

Dr. Adams drove into the lot and parked. He trotted over to them. "What's going on? Oh, wow! How did that happen?"

"The window got broken," Manny said.

"That's obvious! How?" Dr. Adams asked.

Lin started to say "Sam" but shrugged.

"Probably one of the farmers shooting at a coyote or rabbit, and the bullet strayed," Manny said.

"Bullet!" Dr. Adams said. "Do you think—?"

"Don't you start too!" Manny cautioned.

Dr. Adams glanced at Lin and raised his eyebrow as if asking if she agreed.

Lin spun on her heels and walked toward the cafe. She chose a table toward the back of the cafe, as far from the door and window as she could get. She jerked a chair out and plopped into it. Maybe alone is not bad. Especially if the others think she is some sort of neurotic, hysterical woman. If only they had seen Sam and heard him, they would understand and believe her.

The waitress brought a glass of water. "Eating alone?" she asked. She handed Lin a menu. "Save some room for the cobbler tonight."

Manny and Dr. Adams came in and pulled out chairs. "We used a trash bag and some surgical tape; the car should be safe from the weather," Manny said. "I want to take out that bullet casing tomorrow when there's better light. And I want to take a couple of photos too."

Lin said, "Then you believe me?"

Manny grinned. "I didn't say that, but it deserves looking into, Lin. Whoever did this needs to be warned not to aim toward the road when they're hunting."

Lin clicked her tongue against her teeth. "I suppose it depends on what—or whom—they are hunting, Manny." She pretended to study the menu. But she could feel her face warm with anger.

Dr. Adams cleared his throat. "If it's moved on to Manny and Lin, then call me Ric."

Lin looked up at Ric and smiled. "Ric, it is." She avoided looking at Manny. He should know how she felt.

He got the message. "Lin, or do I have to go back to Ms. Hill? Lin, I am an officer of the law. I can't assume things without facts. Give me time to investigate, and I will find the facts. I promise."

Lin leaned back in her chair. "What's good here? I mean, besides the famous cobbler."

"Chicken potpie, Yankee roast beef, the vegetable plate," Ric rattled off. "The veggies are not overcooked. Nice crisp ones. And homemade rolls with them."

The waitress returned. Lin ordered the vegetable plate. The waitress glanced at Manny and Ric. "The usual?"

When there was no protest, she wandered back into the kitchen. She returned with Lin's vegetable plate and rolls, the potpie for the doctor, and the roast beef with mashed potatoes and gravy for Manny.

"The 'usual'?" she asked, smiling. "You get the same thing every night?"

The men shrugged simultaneously. "When you find a good thing, why change it?" Manny said.

Lin couldn't help but wonder if he felt the same way about the job. Would he really pursue this the way she hoped? As they ate, she tried to make idle conversation. What did they do for entertainment around here? Were there interesting spots nearby to visit? What was the main source of living?

It seems that entertainment depended on a satellite dish or a long trip to the nearest real town with a movie house. The interesting spots were limited to the lake where the locals had tried for years to catch a legendary big fish. The main source of living was either light farming, folk art, or living on retirement. So much for Potash.

When the waitress had cleared the table, she brought bowls of cobbler topped with vanilla ice cream. Lin had to admit the reputation was well earned. And despite her mixed feelings about Manny, she was glad to have the company at dinner.

With dinner over, Lin said she was returning to Thelma's.

Ric stood. "I'll follow you back to Thelma's. I'll rest better if I know you are safely there."

"Thank you," Lin said. It was nice to have someone concerned.

"It's early yet," Manny interrupted. "I will be the escort." He said it so emphatically that Ric looked as taken aback as Lin felt.

Manny muttered, "I brought those manuscripts. I thought maybe you'd—"

"Sure," Lin said. *Who knows? Maybe he is a real find.* Perhaps if she showed him some interest in his manuscripts, he would give her problem with Sam more attention.

Ric held up both hands as if surrendering. "Fine, you're right, Manny. If there was danger, what would I defend her with—an injection needle?" He turned to Lin. "I'll see you at Thelma's for breakfast."

"You'll see us both," Manny said, obviously enjoying fending off Ric's attentions to Lin.

She shrugged off their attempts at paying for her meal. She didn't offer to pick up the tab for theirs either. In the parking lot, Lin thanked the doctor for his company and unlocked the driver's side door of her rental car. The ceiling light lit up the interior. She saw that the shattered window was covered with a clear trash bag, and the glass was removed from the cushion and floor. A slight copper metal caught the glint of the light; it was the bullet embedded in the seat back. Lin shuddered involuntarily. She only hoped it was a farmer's stray shot. If Sam knew that she was here, he could react violently.

She drove back to Thelma's. The headlights of Manny's jeep were constantly in her rearview mirror. She pulled into the small parking area, and Manny parked his jeep next to her car. When he got out of the jeep, he was carrying a briefcase.

He followed her to the door and waited while she fished for the key. "You should always have the key ready," he said. "You are too vulnerable when you stand at a door unprepared."

"Thank you for the suggestion," Lin said. Her voice was deliberately cold. She knew that. How vulnerable was she right now with an armed deputy at her side?

As promised, the parlor was well lighted and inviting. Lin dreaded reading the material with the author sitting across from her. It would make Manny nervous, and it definitely made her nervous. Was he expecting her to laugh, shed a tear, what? Every sniff or throat clearing could be misread.

"I can read these before I go to bed," she said. "I can talk with you at breakfast."

Manny shook his head. "Not in front of Ric. He's the only one who knows I am taking the course and trying to write. But I don't want him to be around when you give me the bad news."

Lin sighed, resigned. "Who says it's bad news?" She took the papers offered her and sat in a Queen Anne chair near the Victorian table lamp.

Manny sat on the love seat across from her. Lin braced herself for what she might see. She blinked at the title to be sure she hadn't misread it. "Bobby Bunny's Big Buffet Bash?" she read aloud. "You are writing for children?"

He frowned. "Yes, why?"

"I—I guess I was expecting a hard-boiled detective story or something. It just startled me, that's all," Lin said. "You know, I edit books for adults. I don't feel really qualified to judge children's fiction. It's a very different kind of writing."

"Just tell me what you think. You're a mother. You read to your kid," Manny argued.

Lin nodded. The manuscript was at least short. She'd read this one and tell him she was exhausted. That briefcase looked stuffed, and she didn't want to be reading bunny stories all evening. She leaned toward the light and adjusted the pages so that they were in the best light. She read silently. Lin made it a point to look up and smile at Manny every now and then. The story seemed ridiculous, but he was skillful at expression.

Lin finished and handed the pages back to Manny. His anxious expression made her apprehensive. "Manny, you express yourself well on paper."

A look of disappointment spread across his face. "But?"

Lin cleared her throat. "Yes, there is a but. I am sure that this buffet of foods is useful to young children learning the names of vegetables and fruits. And you are very thorough. I just don't think people will buy it."

Manny's face clouded.

Lin said, "I think that thorough style of yours would be just perfect for a project I have in mind. Would you consider a study of this house and some of the other Revolutionary-age homes around here? I'd really like to have something like that on my list. It would be lots of work. And I can't guarantee that I can buy it, even after all that work. You might have to rewrite it a few times before I would be willing to offer a contract."

"I can do that!" Manny said. "I know I can."

"Think it through and give me your ideas about it. I'll add a few of my own, and we'll see, okay?" Lin stood up and offered her hand. "For now, I need to call in to my ex-in-laws to let them know where I am. I also need to call my son in California."

Grinning, Manny shook her hand and stuffed his manuscript back into the briefcase. "See you tomorrow," he said.

Lin followed him to the door. When he was out, she tested the door to be sure it was locked. Grinning to herself, she climbed the stairs to her room. She had accomplished two things tonight. She had perhaps found a new writer to replace Sam. And she had made sure that Manny would be more willing to investigate Sam and Ben. Surely, life was looking up. She sighed wearily. If she chose to ignore the bullet in her rental car, that is.

CHAPTER 12

When Lin got up to her room, she phoned the auto rental to report the damage to the car. She left a message on their answering machine explaining what had happened. She hoped that would take care of it.

Next she called the Hills. They said that there were no further incidents. This only convinced Lin that Sam knew she was in Potash. He had changed his tactics. She did not mention her troubles. There was no need to worry them.

With the three-hour difference, Jeffrey should be getting ready for bed about now. Lin called him to say good night.

"Kiki took me to Disneyland. I rode everything there. Then Daddy came home and took me to the arcade and we played video games," he told her.

Lin was relieved that he was having such a good time. She would try to hold a good thought for Gerald's wife despite her name. She crawled into bed and slept undisturbed.

The next morning she showered early and was surprised to find Ric and Manny already downstairs in the dining room, enjoying a cup of coffee with Rachel.

Lin sniffed. "Ummmm, cinnamon coffee?"

Rachel smiled. "It's an old restaurant trick. Add cinnamon to the coffee grounds, and no one will ever know if it's fresh ground or not. Oh, this is definitely fresh ground, though."

Rachel went into the kitchen, and Manny and Ric bumped each other, pulling out a chair for Lin. Such attention! She wasn't used to this. Manny seemed quiet. Lin thought perhaps she had upset him last night about his bunny story.

Rachel returned with a platter of mini quiches and fresh cut fruit and went back to the kitchen. In moments she returned with sausage, Canadian bacon, and the rolls. Before she was finished, she added eggs.

Mentally, Lin added up the potential calories and cholesterol. She decided to concentrate on the fruit and quiche. She remembered that Canadian bacon wasn't as big a no-no as regular bacon and took one slice. The men, on the other hand, loaded their plates with something of everything.

They ate instead of talking. Lin had a sense that something was wrong. She also thought she was the only one in the room who didn't have a clue as to what it was. She glimpsed Manny elbow Ric in the ribs.

Ric jumped slightly. "Oh, oh, excuse me. I'll be back in a few minutes." He left the dining room and went into the kitchen. Lin noticed, however, that his shoes were visible where the door didn't quite touch the floor. He remained on the other side, eavesdropping.

Manny pulled a folded paper from his back pocket. He glanced around, hesitating.

"Another manuscript?" Lin asked.

Manny dipped his head. "Er, no. Lin, I really hate to do this, but I don't have a choice. It's a court order. As an officer of the court, I—"

Lin held out her hand. "What on earth? The car rental is holding me liable for the repairs?" She grabbed the paper and unfolded it.

It was a restraining order issued by a county judge. It said that she was not to call or come within 50 feet of Samuel Blessing.

"What? You have got to be kidding! Why? I don't believe this!" Lin said. She tossed the restraining order aside. "I just don't believe this."

"It's legal, and it's binding," Manny said. "If you ignore it, I will have no choice but to arrest you. Lin, please."

"You did this!" Her voice was nearly a shriek. The kitchen door quivered, as if Ric were about to come to her aid. Then it settled back on its hinges.

"I did not do this," Manny said. "Sam had it issued."

Lin tapped the table with her fork. "You know what this means, Manny. Sam knows that I am here. And if he knows, I don't think there's any doubt that he shot at me." A shiver crept up her spine. "He tried to kill me."

Manny shook his head. "I still don't believe that, Lin. I don't believe he tried to kill you. If he did shoot out the window, and I'm not saying that's true, I think it was a warning. I think he just doesn't like your nosing around in what he considers his business."

Lin slammed the fork down on the table. "His business? His business? What about Benjamin?"

"I called him yesterday. He said there is no Ben. And frankly, Lin, I wonder about that too. I would know, wouldn't I?"

The kitchen door swung open, and Ric came in. His face was so red that his freckles melted together. "Uh, everything okay?" he asked. He was looking directly at Lin.

"No, everything is not okay," she said between clenched teeth. "Manny here thinks I'm crazy, I guess."

"Not at all!" Manny protested. "I told you, Lin, I have to deal with facts. Show me the facts."

"Wait here," Lin said. She stalked upstairs and returned with papers. "This is the contract with Benjamin. I brought it to remind him of his commitment—that is, if he is still alive." She looked directly at Manny as she said that.

"Here is Sam's signature as a witness. See? The signatures are nothing alike. How can he deny to you that Benjamin exists when he witnessed his signature?" Lin slipped into her chair across from Manny. "Perhaps he isn't lying. Perhaps Benjamin doesn't exist because he killed him!"

"Manny, maybe you ought to listen to her. She could be right," Ric said.

Manny stood. "I'll keep looking into this, I promise. So far the faxes from surrounding areas haven't produced any information. But I'm still waiting on others. Meanwhile, the restraining order is serious, Lin. Honor it, or I will be forced to arrest you, regardless of how I personally feel." He excused himself. He called out a thank you to Rachel and left.

Lin leaned back. She stirred the food around her plate. She had lost her appetite.

Ric leaned across the table and placed his hand over hers. "Manny is a good cop, an honest one. He'll get to the bottom of this, no matter where it takes him. But take him seriously about the restraining order, Lin." He grinned at her. "I'm not sure I make enough to bail you out!"

Lin shoved her plate aside. "Somebody knows the truth. And I'm going to find that person. This I promise, even if I have to take the entire two weeks of my son's vacation."

"But the judge—"

She snatched up the restraining order and the contract. "Maybe I can't get near Sam. But the order doesn't keep me from his neighbors!" Lin stood, shoving her chair back sharply. "I am not crazy, neurotic, or in any way mentally disturbed. There is a logical explanation for all of this whether it is murder or mind games, and I am going to find out."

Peligroso, that voice was whispering again. Dangerous. She shook it off. There was more danger in not knowing. She would never feel safe again until she knew the truth.

CHAPTER 13

Lin felt as if she were living a nightmare. Why couldn't she wake up? All the evidence was there. Why would Sam have gotten a restraining order against her if he wasn't aware that she was in Potash? Why couldn't Manny see that?

Ric Adams followed her into the parlor. "Lin, you could be putting your life in danger if this Samuel is as bad tempered as you say."

"If?" Lin echoed. "I'm telling the truth. He was always arrogant. Now, with his twin's success and his failure, he has turned desperate."

"I didn't mean to suggest that you weren't telling the truth," Ric protested. "I don't have a way with words the way you and Manny do."

Lin patted his arm. "I consider you a friend, Ric. And I will try not to think ill of Manny. I guess he is just doing his job. The same way I was doing mine when I rejected Samuel."

"Then you'll let Manny handle this?" Ric asked. His boyish face looked so hopeful that Lin smiled at him.

"I won't do anything to put myself in harm's way," she promised.

The moment Ric left, Lin rushed back upstairs. There was no harm in visiting people who just happened to live on the same road as the Blessing farm. She would not put herself in harm's way. Lin unplugged the cellular phone from its recharge and stuffed it into her briefcase. She grabbed her keys and purse and took the stairs down two at a time. Her tennis shoes made soft thudding sounds against the bare wood.

Lin stuck her head inside the kitchen and complimented Rachel on the breakfast. "I'm off on some sightseeing and fact-gathering," she said. "I don't expect anyone to call for me, but you can just tell them that I'll be in touch."

As Lin unlocked the car door, it occurred to her how ridiculous the locked door was. Anyone who wanted to get in could just go through the broken window. She froze. What if Sam realized she was staying at Thelma's? After all, it was the only place nearby. Sam was capable of anything. She knelt and looked under the car. She half expected to see a bomb. She let her breath out in a wheeze. *Lin, you watch too many crash-and-burn movies,* she told herself. *Get real!*

The sun played hide-and-seek through the heavy stands of trees as Lin drove back toward Potash. She stopped at the gravel road and read the mailboxes: Hayslip, Marsh, Collins, Blessing. She turned onto the gravel road. The first property was that of the Hayslips. Lin turned into the long dirt drive and drove toward the sage green farmhouse. Two shepherd dogs raced up to the car, barking furiously, their tails high and wagging and their ears forward and alert. Lin stopped the car, unsure of what to do.

A woman's head popped up from behind a row of flowers. "Jake, Sadie, come!"

The two dogs raced back toward her, their tongues hanging out. They danced around her as she walked toward the car. "They won't hurt you," she said. "They're all bark and no bite." She held a small spade in one hand. With the other, she patted the dogs.

Hesitantly, Lin got out of the car. "Mrs. Hayslip?"

"Yes, and you are—?"

Lin extended her hand. "Belinda Mendoza Hill. Call me Lin, please. I am researching this area and noticed your name on a mailbox. It caught my attention because it seems so appropriate for a farm family. May we talk a little about the area?"

"Hannah," Mrs. Hayslip said. "Call me Hannah. Come on inside. I'll wash some of this dirt off and we can have some tea. Cranberry tea all right with you?"

"That would be wonderful," Lin said, "but please don't go to any trouble."

Hannah said, "The kettle is always on for company."

Lin followed her into the house, past the living room filled with early American maple furniture and gingham curtains. They walked into a large kitchen painted the same sage green as the outside. Hannah motioned toward the table. "Sit. I'll pour. Then I'll try to answer any questions I can."

She brought mugs of tea to the table. "Guess it's a bit early for cookies, but I have some shortbread."

"Oh, no, thank you! I just finished breakfast at Thelma's," Lin replied. She lifted the mug to her lips and sipped. She didn't want to alarm Hannah, so she began with a simple question. "How long have you lived here?"

"All my life. That is, I was a Collins before I married Ezra. We were neighbors and schoolmates. We've been married nearly 50 years now. Two sons, three daughters, twelve grandchildren, and three great-grandchildren."

Lin nodded and made appropriate sounds of appreciation. "Has the area changed much in that time?"

"No, we're far enough from the cities and not attractive enough for the yuppies, so blessedly we are about the same," Hannah said. "Except for satellite dishes and dishwashers, of course." She laughed.

Lin took another sip. "Do the neighbors socialize much? I noticed other names—Marsh," she said, "Blessing."

Hannah took in a deep breath and let it out slowly. She turned her head toward the window, where the sun cut a bright streak into the room. "Used to. Still do with the Marshes. See them at church mostly. And of course, my brother and his brood live on our old Collins place."

"Blessing?" Lin repeated. She hoped she wasn't being too obvious.

Hannah turned back to squint at her. Lin squirmed uncomfortably. She felt as if Hannah was seeing inside her mind.

"That Samuel doesn't talk much to anyone. Almost a hermit. He's a famous writer, you know. Guess either he's too busy with his books, or he thinks he's too good for the rest of us. His folks were nice, though. Buried at Weeping Willow Cemetery. Lots of patriots buried there."

"Sounds as if I should visit there," Lin agreed. "What about Benjamin Blessing?"

"Yes, he and the missus, both buried there. Ben died in—let me see—1985, and the missus a year later. Grieved herself to death, I suppose."

"I meant Ben Junior, I guess," Lin blurted out. She immediately regretted being so direct.

Hannah Hayslip narrowed her eyes and studied Lin. "Who did you say you were? Why are you asking these questions?"

Lin felt her hands tremble. She grasped the mug tightly. "I—I said I was researching the area. Lin Hill. I may do a book on the area."

"Young lady, I think I've said about all there is to say. Stay away from that Samuel Blessing. He is a bad man. He shot at my dogs because they got a little curious about his diggings."

Lin would have thanked her and left immediately, but she was not sure her legs would hold her. "Diggings?"

"The other night, floodlights glaring and that bulldozer going half the night. You'd think he could've waited till daylight. Who needs to work on a manure pile in the middle of the night? Jake and Sadie just scratched at it a little the next day, and the fool ran them off with his shotgun. Stay away from him. Don't trust anyone who is unkind to animals."

"Manure pile?" Lin repeated dumbly. At midnight? No one would do that, unless he didn't want to be observed. She had a terrible feeling that somewhere in those "diggings," as Hannah called them, was the body of Benjamin.

CHAPTER
14

The sun was well up above the trees when Lin pulled out of the Hayslips' drive and onto the gravel road. Was there a point to visiting the Collinses or Marshes now? She had been too anxious in her questioning of Hannah Hayslip. Hannah was probably already on the phone to the others. Besides, she had learned something important, something terrifying. Samuel had been digging in the middle of the night. Now she had something to take to Manny. He might not believe her, but he would certainly believe one of his own.

Manny was probably already *fishing*. She had failed to get his beeper number. Lin decided to go to Ric's. He was a friend. He would believe her.

A four-wheel drive and a compact car were parked in front of the doctor's house. Lin parked the car and rang the bell. The buzzer sounded, and she entered. She nodded to the man who was waiting, sat down on the sofa, and picked up an old magazine.

The door to the examination room opened, and a woman came out with a baby in her arms. Ric looked surprised at seeing Lin. "Come on in, Mr. Reynolds. I'll be with you in a moment."

When Mr. Reynolds was in the room and Ric had shut the door, he came over to Lin. "You look pale. What is it?"

Lin shook her head. "Not now. Not with someone else here."

"Go back to the kitchen. Get some orange juice from the fridge. You look badly in need of some vitamin C right now. This won't take long."

When Ric had gone into the examination room, Lin got up and went into the kitchen. She felt lost, detached almost. It was as if she were in a twilight zone of sorts.

She finished the glass of juice as Ric came in. He sat across from her and put his hand on her arm. "Now, Lin. What is it? You look as if you've seen a ghost."

Lin took a deep breath. "No, but I may know where one is. That is, I think I know where Benjamin is."

"I'm listening."

"I had a visit with Hannah Hayslip this morning. She said Samuel was using a bulldozer on a big pile of manure."

"The farmers use manure to fertilize their crops. That's not anything to be concerned about."

Lin pulled her arm from Ric's grip and slammed her fist against the table. "In the middle of the night? Under floodlights? He's murdered Benjamin. He's buried him right there on the farm, Ric. I'm sure of it."

"Middle of the night? It does raise the suspicions, Lin. Of course, you need to tell Manny." Ric went to his wall phone and dialed. He turned toward Lin. "He is probably out running down clues now." He paused and grinned. "Or fishing."

They sat, waiting. In a few minutes the doorbell rang. Ric pushed the button to allow the visitor to enter and left Lin in the kitchen. She recognized the voice as Manny's. He looked disturbed as he entered the kitchen.

"Ric says you have some evidence. Lin, I thought you understood the restraining order. What have you been up to?"

"I have obeyed the restraining order," she protested. "I visited with Hannah Hayslip. She said that Samuel was digging out behind the barn in the middle of the night. Manny, you know what that means! He's murdered Ben, and he has buried him on the farm. Now do you believe me?"

Manny rubbed his temples. "Lin, I told you, it isn't a matter of believing or not believing you. I have to have facts."

Lin pushed her chair back and stood. "Your facts are buried on the farm. Can't you get a search warrant?"

"Based on what? That a man chose to labor at night on his own land instead of in the hot sun? If Hannah had called in a complaint about the noise, that would be different. But she didn't."

"Talk to her now, Manny. She'll tell you just as she told me."

Manny frowned. "I talked to Mrs. Marsh. Samuel came to her and asked for the box her new dishwasher came in."

"That is big enough for a body, Manny," Ric said. "It does raise suspicion, doesn't it?"

Lin was grateful for Ric. He at least was willing to consider the possibility for further investigation.

Manny folded his arms and rocked back and forth on his feet. He stared at the ceiling as if deep in thought. It seemed to Lin like an eternity before he spoke. "First of all, you have not proven that there is or ever was a

Benjamin Blessing. Nobody seems to know him. You are the only one."

Lin clenched her teeth. "How dare you! I am not crazy! It's Samuel who is crazy. Why won't you believe me?" Tears of frustration trickled down her cheeks. It made Lin even angrier that she would cry in front on them. She leaned back in the chair. "I am telling you the truth."

She felt as if she were six years old again. A farm owner's daughter once gave Lin a doll. It had dark hair and brown eyes just as she did. The father accused Lin of stealing it. No matter how much she protested, the man wouldn't believe her. His daughter was afraid of him and kept silent. Lin felt so alone, so ashamed, although she had nothing to be ashamed of. That's just how she felt now too—alone and ashamed.

"I will check around," Manny said. "I'll ask a few questions. But everything can probably be explained away."

Lin looked Manny squarely in the eye. "The packing box?"

"Storing old clothes perhaps."

"The digging?"

"Catching up with his chores."

"The shattered window?"

"What goes up must come down. Even if it was Samuel—and I am not saying it was—he could have fired into the air."

Lin sighed. Even if he could discover that Sam's gun had been fired recently, there was Hannah Hayslip who would say he had fired at her dogs. Nothing she said made any impact on Manny.

Ric said, "I have an idea! Let's go to the cafe. It's pizza day. Maybe by the time we have some food in us, we'll have some ideas."

Reluctantly, Lin walked out to the front. She was in no

mood to eat with someone who didn't believe anything she said. "You want to go in the rental car?" she asked unhappily.

"I have to go in the patrol, just in case," Manny said.

"I'll ride with you, Lin," Ric said.

Lin unlocked the passenger door and opened it. A piece of paper on the seat caught her eye. It was a typed note. It said, "LET IT GO."

Ric said, "I'll get Manny!"

Lin shook her head. "Never mind," she said. "He'd just say I probably typed it myself. Or it was meant for someone else. Or it was about something else. Until I prove to him that Benjamin is real—wait a minute! I have an idea. The Blessings have lived here all their lives. The doctor at that time probably delivered Samuel and Benjamin. Wouldn't there be records?"

"I have all the files from the previous doctor," Ric said. "But I couldn't let you see them, not without a release from a living relative. Unfortunately, that's Sam."

"Ric, you have got to help me. Surely, there is a way to get past Sam."

"Absolutely not!" Ric said but he grinned mischievously. "However, I am in grave need of someone to alphabetize and clean up my files. Now if you are willing to—"

Lin hugged Ric. "You're the greatest!" She pulled back, embarrassed. "Sorry. I just got carried away."

Ric grinned. "Don't apologize. Now let's meet Manny. And let's make this our little secret," he said. "Otherwise, he'll probably think of a reason you can't do it."

Lin went around to the driver's side and slid behind the wheel. She felt lighter as if she'd just thrown a big sack of troubles off her back. Once she had proof that there was a twin, Manny would have to believe her.

CHAPTER 15

Lin wished she could gobble down lunch and get on to "alphabetizing" Ric Adams' patient files. She glanced at Ric several times during lunch, and an involuntary smile crept across her face. He grinned back at her with all the air of a kid who knew a secret.

Manny's right eyebrow shot up as he looked from one to the other. "What's up? You two cats have canaries before we got here?"

Did he think that she and Ric were—? Lin felt her face flush. "Uh, I was just thinking how similar pizza is to a taco. Guess I was wondering if there are parallels in other cultures."

"It's a great idea," Ric said. "Eat the plate and there are no dishes to wash. There are egg rolls in Chinese cuisine."

"What about blintzes?" Manny added. "Pigs in a blanket, hot dogs, hamburgers?"

Lin laughed, grateful that the conversation had drifted

in a safe direction. "And pierogies. It would make a wonderful cookbook. We could call it *No-Plate Meals*."

"Or *I Hate Plates Cookbook*," Ric said. "Or *Eat Your Plate Meals*."

"I could do that!" Manny said.

Lin smiled. "Stick to the Revolutionary homes project," she told him. "If you did a cookbook, we might have to give you a pen name, like Granny Manny."

The three of them laughed so hard, the other patrons of the cafe turned to stare. Lin was relieved when it was time to drive Ric back to the clinic and Manny's beeper called him to duty. Someone's milk cow had broken through a fence and was trampling Mrs. Rankin's garden.

Back at the clinic, Ric opened a door to what may have been a utility room at one time. Now it held file cabinets.

"I'll go scrub down the examination room," Ric said. "What I don't see I won't know. And what I won't know can't get either of us in trouble." He grinned. "I hope," he added.

When he had left, Lin opened the first cabinet, marked A-C. As soon as she saw the files, though, she realized they were not in alphabetical order. She pulled a chair into the room and sat down. This was going to be tedious and time-consuming.

It was nearly 3 P.M. when she came across the files: Blessing, Benjamin Sr. Blessing, Ann Houseman. Blessing, Samuel. She abandoned her alphabetizing and quickly thumbed through the remaining files until she pulled out Blessing, Benjamin Jr.

Lin snatched up the four files and clutched them to her, sighing with great relief. She hurried into the parlor. The door to the examination room was open. There were no patients. "Ric!" she called. "I found him! I found Ben!"

Ric came out, stripping plastic gloves from his hands. "Great!" As he opened the files, his face turned cloudy. "According to this, Samuel Blessing was a single birth."

"No!" Lin said. "Look, right there is Benjamin. The old doctor just kept a different filing system, that's all."

Ric handed one file back to Lin. "According to this, Benjamin Blessing was a stillborn five years prior to Samuel's birth."

"This is crazy! There has to be some mistake!" Lin said. She realized she was shrieking like some hysterical woman in a horror movie. *Calm down,* she told herself. *Take a deep breath and calm down. Relax.* She swallowed hard. "Ric, it was not unusual for parents to name a second child after a deceased one. I will look some more. Do you have other file cabinets?"

Ric shook his head. "I'm telling you, Lin, this says that Samuel was a single birth. There is no twin named Benjamin."

Lin sank into a chair. "I have not been working with a ghost, Ric. I have worked with both Sam and Ben for years. I am not crazy. But I think maybe Sam is trying to drive me there."

Ric left and returned with a glass of water and a small round tablet. "Take this, doctor's orders. You are shaking. We will figure this out. I believe you, Lin."

"But Manny doesn't! And I was counting on your files to prove me right. I mean, I have seen Benjamin. He is nothing like Sam except in looks. He's outgoing, cheerful, has a wonderful mind that can create witty plots. They are raunchy books, but they are so popular. Sam is quick tempered, arrogant, tedious with his detail but a wonderful researcher. Neither of them came in very often to hand deliver their manuscripts. Mostly they mailed them." Lin leaped up. "Mail! The post office! Ric, surely the postmaster has seen them plenty of times. He will tell Manny!"

Ric shrugged. Lin was not sure he was going along with her anymore. He glanced at his watch. "It's 4 P.M. The post office is in the grocery store. It'll be closing soon. I'll close up and take you there."

The tranquilizer Ric had given her was beginning to calm Lin. The post office was her last chance to prove that there was a Benjamin Blessing. She realized she might have to leave this village defeated. And what would become of her at home? Would Sam leave her alone? Would he threaten Jeffrey? Couldn't anyone see that he was dangerous?

The bell above the door jangled as they entered the grocer's. Ric took Lin by the arm and led her to a partitioned corner with a cage-like window. Brass letters on it said "United States Postal Station, Potash. Lawrence Dawson, Postmaster."

Ric rang the small bell on the counter, and a white-haired man with a balloon-like stomach waddled toward them. "Hey, Doc Adams. Expecting a package?"

"No, Larry, but this is Lin Hill, and she'd like to ask you something."

"I'll answer if I can, ma'am."

"Do you know Samuel Blessing?" she asked.

"Oh, yes. He's a famous author, you know. Mails his manuscripts right here." He tapped the counter. "A bit of a snob, but then I guess being famous and all . . ."

Lin hesitated. "Lawrence Dawson, Larry Dawson. Didn't Benjamin Blessing dedicate a book to you?"

Larry face brightened. "You saw that?"

Lin grinned. "I was the editor."

"Let me shake your hand. That's wonderful!" he said.

Lin glanced back at Ric to be sure he was listening. "How did you know the author?" she asked.

"Why, he comes here to mail his manuscripts. Said he didn't trust leaving it in the mailbox for pickup." He tapped the counter. "Laid it right here. Trusted it into my hands. Nice man. Not like his brother at all. I don't think they have much to do with each other. Jealousy is a terrible thing. Benjamin is always laughing, Samuel is always fussing about one thing or another. Never saw Benjamin much, though. Think he probably kept his nose to the computer."

Lin felt light-headed, and it wasn't the tranquilizer. She had found someone here who admitted to knowing both Benjamin and Samuel!

Ric clasped his hand over hers. "I guess that means good news and bad news," he said. "The good news is that you are right." He sighed. "The bad news is that you are right, and we could be dealing with a killer."

CHAPTER
16

Lin felt relieved and scared. Some secret part of her had wished she was wrong. Yet she was glad that Ric and Manny wouldn't think she was the crazy one.

Ric glanced at his watch. "Larry, would you page Manny for us, please? Tell him to meet us right here."

"When he comes, please tell him the same thing you told me," Lin added.

* * *

Manny arrived and heard Larry explain how he knew Benjamin. Then Manny said, "I'll go to Hannah Hayslip's right now. I'll talk her into making a formal complaint about the noise. I'll take that to the night judge at the county seat. It could be late, but I am sure he'll give me a warrant with what I know now." He turned to leave but turned back. "Lin, I'm sorry."

She nodded, relieved. "Well, now you have the facts you need, Manny. You don't have to believe me."

Lin thanked Larry, and she and Ric went to the cafe to wait for Manny to return from the county seat. When he returned, he told the waitress to brew them up some thermoses of coffee and make a few sandwiches. It could be a long night.

"Ric, I'll need you as coroner."

Lin said, "What about me? What about the restraining order? Can't I come too?"

"The restraining order has been revoked at my request," Manny said. "Do you think you are up to this? It could be pretty upsetting."

Lin tapped the table with her fingers. "Maybe you think all of this hasn't been upsetting! Yes, I'm up to it, Manny. I have to see this through."

As they drove to the Blessing farm, Manny told them, "I have several of the deputies meeting us there. They will wait at the crossroads, though, so as not to give warning. We don't know what Sam's reaction will be, and we want to be prepared. Until he is under the watchful eye of a deputy, Lin, I want you to stay in the patrol jeep. Understood?"

"Understood," she agreed. She felt a tingling over her body. Her adrenaline had kicked in full force.

Several patrol vehicles were parked near the mailboxes at the crossroads. They did not use their sirens, but they turned on their flashing lights as they drove down the gravel road.

The three cars turned under the arch that said Blessing Farm and headed toward the house. Sam stood there, his arms folded across his chest and a shotgun. His eyes looked dark with anger. "What is *she* doing here? There's a restraining order against her!"

"Revoked," Manny said. He handed him a piece of paper. "This is a warrant to search your place, including the dirt and manure pile behind your barn."

"No!" Sam said. "You can't do that!"

"This paper says we can." He nodded toward the other deputies, and they trotted toward the rear with portable floodlights and shovels.

"Hand me the shotgun, Sam," Manny said. "It is possible evidence in a shooting incident last evening."

Sam shoved the shotgun toward Manny. He glared at Lin. "I should have killed her!"

Manny took the weapon. "This is a good time to tell you that you are under arrest for attempted murder. By the time we are finished digging, charges will possibly be raised to murder. Anything you say may be held against you. You are entitled to an attorney. If you cannot afford an attorney, one will be appointed on your behalf . . ."

"I only wanted to scare her! And there is no murder. There is no Benjamin!"

Manny said, "Sam, put one hand on your head and the other behind your back." He cuffed the hand behind Sam's back. Then he pulled the other hand behind Sam and snapped the cuffs on that one. He led him around to the rear of the barn. Lin followed them with Ric steadying her.

The floodlights were shining on the pile of manure. The deputies were at the sides of the pile digging. "I hit something!" one of them called.

The others abandoned their spots and joined the one. Within minutes they had uncovered a large box with "Whirlpool Dishwasher, This Side Up" printed on it.

Lin shivered as they pried open the box.

"What the—?" one of them shouted. "Manny! Come here. You gotta see this!"

"Are you sure you're up to this?" Ric asked.

Lin nodded solemnly. "Just don't let go of my hand, please."

The deputies parted to let Ric and Lin and Manny approach.

Lin braced herself and covered her nose and mouth in expectation. She had to do this. She had to for Benjamin's sake. For her family's sake. She looked into the box and felt her knees go weak. Staring blankly up at her, atop a small pile of ashes, was Jeffrey's teddy bear.

Manny shook his head in disbelief. He turned to one of the deputies. "Get those ashes into an evidence bag. I want them analyzed."

Lin's thoughts were scrambled like the morning eggs. "I think I know what the ashes are." She looked at Sam. "Benjamin's manuscript. Am I right?"

Sam laughed. "You'll never have it now! I told you you'd be sorry!"

"But Benjamin?"

"Don't you get it, you dense woman? I *was* Benjamin! I *am* Samuel! Intelligence can always defeat the pathetically stupid." He turned to Manny. "Now get these ridiculous cuffs off me!"

"You still have attempted murder and disturbing the peace here, breaking and entering, vandalism, and threatening your editor in New York City." He glanced toward the teddy bear. "And theft. So you aren't going anywhere but to jail."

"And to the nearest mental facility for evaluation," Ric whispered to Lin.

The deputies turned off all but one of the floodlights. They led Sam to one of the patrol jeeps and put him inside. Manny, Lin, and Ric walked back toward Manny's four-wheel drive.

"I don't get it," Lin said. "Is he a multiple personality, or is he just an egotistical egghead who wrote trash for a living and was embarrassed to admit it? He was jealous of himself?"

"Whichever he is, the courts and psychiatrists will argue it out, Lin," Ric said. "And either way, I think he is out of your hair for good."

As Lin started to climb into Manny's patrol, she heard her name called, "Lin! Lin! Over here!" She looked back to see Sam's face at the window of a deputy's jeep. "When we get all this straightened out," he said, "how would you like to see a manuscript from my brother James? He writes great science fiction!"

Without answering, Lin climbed into Manny's vehicle. Ric slid in next to her. She looked over at Manny, who started the engine.

"I hate this cliché from every horror film I've seen," Lin said, smiling, "but let's get out of here!"